"You want me to follow her?"

Todd asked.

Again, his boss squirmed. "Not exactly," he hedged. "What you're to do is find a way to meet her and get friendly."

Todd tensed. "How friendly?" His tone was icy.

"As friendly as you have to be to gain her confidence. You know what I'm talking about, and you're in for a treat. This is one gorgeous lady."

The man took several black-and-white photographs from the folder and handed them across the desk to Todd.

Todd studied the pictures. Dinah Swensen was not only incredibly beautiful, but there was a magnetic sexiness that radiated from the photographs and tweaked him in the pit of his stomach.

A sick feeling of distaste for the job assailed him, and he glared at Wesley Nelson. "If you're saying that you want me to seduce this woman to get information, then you'll have to find someone else. I'm an investigator, not a stud."

Dear Reader,

May . . . the month when flowers—and love—are in full bloom—especially here at Silhouette Romance. And as you know, spring is also that special time of year when a man's thoughts turn to love. Be they the boy next door or a handsome, mysterious stranger, our heroes are no exception! Six lucky heroines are about to find their dreams of happy-ever-after come true as once again, Silhouette Romance sweeps you away with heartwarming, poignant stories of love.

In the months to come, we'll be publishing romances by many of your all-time favorites, including Diana Palmer, Brittany Young and Annette Broadrick. And coming next month, Nora Roberts will launch her not-to-be-missed Calhoun Women Series with the June Silhouette Romance, *Courting Catherine*.

WRITTEN IN THE STARS is a very special event for 1991. Each month, we're proud to present a Silhouette Romance that focuses on the hero—and his astrological sign. May features the stubborn-but-loveable Taurus man. Our authors and editors have created this delightfully romantic series especially for you, the reader, and we'd love to hear what you think. After all, at Silhouette Romance, we take our readers' comments to heart!

Please write to us at Silhouette Romance
                       300 East 42nd Street
                       New York, New York
                       10017

We look forward to hearing from you!

Sincerely,

Valerie Susan Hayward
Senior Editor

PHYLLIS HALLDORSON

Lady Diamond

Silhouette Romance

Published by Silhouette Books New York

America's Publisher of Contemporary Romance

For Tara Hughes Gavin
Indispensible as my sometimes editor.
Cherished as my dear friend.

SILHOUETTE BOOKS
300 E. 42nd St., New York, N.Y. 10017

LADY DIAMOND

ISBN: 0-373-08791-8

First Silhouette Books printing May 1991

Printed in the U.S.A.

PHYLLIS HALLDORSON

At age sixteen, Phyllis Halldorson met her real-life Prince Charming. She married him a year later, and they settled down to raise a family. A compulsive reader, Phyllis dreamed of someday finding the time to write stories of her own. That time came when her two youngest children reached adolescence. When she was introduced to romance novels, she knew she had found her long-delayed vocation. After all, how could she write anything else after living all those years with her very own Silhouette hero?

Chapter One

Todd Campbell almost made it out of the cubicle he laughingly called an office at the firm of Halliburton & Associates, Professional Investigators, before the phone rang. He swore softly and glanced at the clock on the wall. Almost six-thirty—well past quitting time. He took a couple more steps before his conscience caught up with him, and with a sigh he turned around to go back and answer it.

"Campbell, glad I caught you," said the gruff voice of his superior, Wesley Nelson, through the receiver. "Stop in my office before you leave. I have an assignment for you."

Todd muttered an old cliché about Lincoln freeing the slaves as he put the phone in its cradle, but as a very junior member of this new and upscale firm of yuppie private investigators in Los Angeles, he was in no position to refuse. At age twenty-five he was five years younger than the next oldest operative and therefore got all the cases no one else wanted.

A few minutes later, he entered Nelson's office and the other man stood to greet him from behind the cluttered desk. "Sorry to delay you, Todd," he said, "but we got this case late this afternoon, and we need someone on it right away."

Todd groaned inwardly, but tried to be understanding as he asked if he could use the phone to postpone a date.

"Better cancel it," Wes said ominously.

"Oh, hell," Todd said as he ran his fingers through his light blond hair and was reminded by the length of it that he'd better make an early appointment with his hairstylist. "I guess you'd better tell me what I'm getting into before I do anything else."

Wes sat back down and opened a file folder. "First I have to know if you're free to travel. You do have a summer break from those night classes you're taking at that private law school, don't you?"

Todd perked up. Travel? Sounded interesting. "Yes," he confirmed. "I'm out of school until September. Why?"

Wes nodded his approval, then picked up a paper from the folder. "Six years ago there was a two-million-dollar jewel heist in one of those jewelry stores on Rodeo Drive where you have to make an appointment to shop. One of the employees, a thirty-year-old man named Anson Erhardt, was arrested and later convicted, but they never recovered the gems. Erhardt insisted he was innocent and knew nothing about anything. Now he's up for parole next month, and the insurance company has hired us to find them."

Todd's interest escalated. It sounded as if they were giving him a real case at last. "You want me to follow him?"

Wes shifted uncomfortably. "Well, no. We'll have someone else do that if necessary once he's released. What

I didn't mention is that he has, or rather *had,* a wife. Name's Dinah, but the police could never connect her with the robbery. She stood by him until he was convicted, then divorced him, took back her maiden name of Swensen, and moved to Arizona.''

Todd frowned. ''I don't understand,'' he said, but he was afraid that he did, and he didn't like it.

''The point is,'' said Wes, ''that the insurance investigators believe that she either has the stones or knows where they are. They figure that the divorce was just a blind to make everyone think she was the naive innocent she pretended to be. Meanwhile she's got the gems stashed away somewhere, and once Erhardt is free, they'll take them and leave the country.''

''Then you want me to follow her?'' Todd asked.

Again Wes squirmed. ''Not exactly,'' he hedged. ''What you're to do is find a way to meet her and get friendly.''

Todd tensed. ''How friendly?'' His tone was icy.

Wes stopped fidgeting and sat up straight, assuming an air of authority. ''As friendly as you have to be to gain her confidence. You know what I'm talking about, man, and you're in for a treat. This is one gorgeous lady.''

He took several black-and-white photographs from the folder and handed them across the desk to Todd. ''She was twenty-seven when these were taken by the news photographers at the time of the trial. She's thirty-two now but still blond with big blue eyes and curves that would make any man itch.''

He winked. ''You've got it made, kid. She's older than you and she looks cool, but there's bound to be a lot of passion simmering under that composure. She works for a property-management firm in Phoenix, Arizona, and word has it that she hasn't been seriously involved with a man since she's been there.''

Todd studied the pictures and silently agreed that Wes's description was accurate. Dinah Swensen was not only incredibly beautiful, but there was a magnetic sexiness that radiated from the black-and-white photographs and tweaked him in the pit of his stomach.

A sick feeling of distaste for the job assailed him, and he glared at Wesley Nelson. "If you're saying that you want me to seduce this woman to get information, then you'll have to find someone else. I'm an investigator, not a stud."

He stood and turned his back on the other man as he strode toward the door.

"Todd, damm it, come back here and quit acting like an outraged virgin!" Wes bellowed angrily. "For God's sake, I don't care how you get the information from her, just *get it*. If you can do it by taking her to church, or buying her hot fudge sundaes at the local ice-cream parlor then fine, but we have to find those gems and you'd better not screw up. Understand?"

The ring of the telephone and the chime of the doorbell sounding simultaneously didn't surprise Dinah Swensen, considering how things had been going lately. Being resident manager for a big apartment complex filled with middle-income families was a twenty-four-hour-a-day job that hardly left her time to sleep, let alone oversee the three apartment buildings she also managed in the surrounding area.

She let the answering machine pick up the incoming call while she headed for the door. This would be the applicant she was scheduled to interview for the position of lifeguard. At least it wouldn't take long, because if he were under eighty and could swim, she'd hire him. The myriad of kids in the complex had been driving her crazy to reopen the pool since she'd had to close it when the former lifeguard quit two days earlier without notice in order to take a better-paying job.

The chime sounded again just before she reached the door. Dinah pulled it open, then stared. Even through the screen she could see that this guy was a magnificent hunk! Sun-bleached blond hair cut short with a mass of soft curls on top, warm brown eyes and a drop-dead physique. He wore tight jeans which pulled across a flat stomach and encased muscular thighs that rippled when he moved. His broad shoulders and chest were covered with a white T-shirt, and his bare arms were definitely those of a swimmer, with long streamlined muscles.

A wide smile lit his handsome face. "Ms. Swensen?" he asked in a voice that could only be described as lower-register tenor, young and sexy.

Dinah blinked and tried to disguise the embarrassment she felt at being caught gawking like a teenager. "Yes, I'm Dinah Swensen," she said briskly. "You must be Mr. Campbell."

"Todd," he insisted as she unlocked the screen door and let him in. "I understand you need a lifeguard."

"Do I ever." She sighed as she motioned him to the blue-and-rose flowered chair that matched the sofa. "The one I had suddenly quit and I had to close the pool. We have about a hundred kids of all ages living here who are out of school now and want to swim all day. I'm going to have a riot on my hands if I don't open it soon, so I hope you're available. Can I get you something to drink? Soda? Iced tea? Lemonade?"

He continued to stand. "Thank you. Soda will be fine. This desert sun is hot."

Since the living room, dining room and kitchen comprised the front half of the apartment and all opened into one another, Dinah could see and talk to him while she filled two glasses with ice and cola. "Have you worked as a lifeguard before?" she asked.

He nodded. "Yeah. That's how I put myself through college."

Her eyes widened. "You're a college graduate? Then why on earth are you applying for this job?"

He looked a little sheepish. "I graduated from a state college in Florida a year ago after going part-time for six years. Starting this fall I'll be attending law school at the university in Tempe, and I'd rather pay my way through as a lifeguard than wait tables."

A wave of admiration swept over Dinah as she walked into the living room and handed him one of the two glasses, then sat down on the sofa. It was only then that he sat, too.

"I . . . I can't tell you how much I respect you for being willing to work so hard for an education," she said. It wasn't often she met a young man with so much ambition.

For a moment he looked disconcerted, and when he spoke, he was almost abrupt. "I'm not a hero, Dinah. It was simply a matter of wanting an education and being willing to work for it."

For a moment she was startled by his brusqueness, but then his dazzling smile was back. "Besides, I love water sports. Some of my college credits were in boating, swimming and waterskiing. If you hire me, I can start right away because I have all the necessary certificates and credentials."

Dinah smiled with pure relief. "In that case, as of now you're our new lifeguard."

Then a thought occurred to her, and the smile dimmed. "Seriously though, Todd, I have to tell you that if I had a choice, I'd choose a young man who was less...spectacular looking."

Todd eyed her inquiringly. "I beg your pardon?"

She could feel the hot flush that stained her face. "Oh, come on now," she reproved. "You know very well that you're going to have every female in the place, both mothers and daughters, swarming around that pool, vying for your attention. A lot of them will even pretend to be in trouble, so you'll have to rescue them. A kid as handsome as you can cause more problems than he solves. Especially when he works in a bathing suit."

Just the thought of Todd Campbell in a pair of skimpy trunks sent a shiver down her spine.

For a moment there was silence, then it was Todd who broke it.

"I'm not a kid, Dinah," he said firmly. "I'm a twenty-five-year-old man, and I resent your referring to me as one every bit as much as you'd resent it if I called you a girl. I can't help the way I look, but neither do I flirt with the female swimmers I'm supposed to be protecting. I've had plenty of experience handling those situations, and I promise to keep them under control."

Now she was truly mortified. She hadn't meant to insult him!

To her relief he changed the subject. "I understand you're the resident manager here. Do you have an apartment I could rent?"

"You want to live *here?*" she asked, surprised.

"Well, yeah. I'm temporarily sharing a place with three other guys, but it's on the other side of Phoenix. This is a great location. I won't have to leave the grounds to go to work, and it's only a short drive to the university."

"I'm sorry," she said regretfully, "but we rent only to families with children."

He raised one inquiring eyebrow. "Oh? Isn't that discrimination?"

Dinah felt her hackles rise. "Yes, I suppose it is, but it's nothing compared to the discrimination that goes on *against* children. Our tenants are blue-collar workers who make too much money to qualify for federal subsidies and not enough to swing the huge down payment on a house by themselves. They're not poor by any means, but in today's inflated economy they fall between the cracks and nobody seems to care."

Dinah didn't realize that she'd raised her voice until Todd held up both hands in a gesture of defeat. "Hey, I'm sorry." His tone was part amused and part serious. "I didn't mean to offend you. I didn't know it was a sin to try to rent an apartment here unless I had a houseful of kids."

Again she was embarrassed. What was there about this young man that rattled her so?

"No, I'm the one who's sorry," she apologized. "I overreacted, but being in the real-estate business is a real eye-opener. You'd be surprised at how many ways there are to turn away couples with children without getting in trouble for it. This place is set up specifically for kids. We have a playground, a wading pool as well as the big one, and even a child-care center for infants through third grade."

She smiled. "You wouldn't want to live here. This place is a madhouse most of the time. I assure you, we've never had couples without children banging at the doors to get in."

He leaned forward. "I'm sure you haven't, but I'm used to kids. They wouldn't bother me. I don't need a whole apartment, just a place to sleep and a microwave oven to heat up a meal now and then. Surely you have an extra room somewhere."

Dinah hesitated. Now that he'd mentioned it, she remembered that there was a room that could be made available to him, but how had he known?

She shook her head to dislodge that silly thought. Of course he hadn't known; he'd just described what he needed, and she happened to have something that would be suitable.

"There's a large storage room in the recreation building that could be cleaned out and fixed up," she said slowly. "I can't rent it on a long-term basis, but you can stay there for a month or two until you find more suitable quarters. You'd have to furnish it yourself since all our units are rented unfurnished, and the only bathrooms are the public ones, but I can let you have it for a nominal fee."

"I'll take it," he said without a pause.

"But you haven't even seen it," she protested.

He exhaled and relaxed against the back of the chair. "Yeah, you're right, I'd better look at it, but I'm sure it will do nicely."

An hour later, Todd Campbell drove the run-down secondhand Ford, that he'd bought as soon as he'd arrived in Phoenix four days before, toward the hotel where he was staying. The radio blared soft rock, but even that couldn't take his mind off the woman he'd just left.

He wouldn't have believed it possible, but Dinah Swensen was even more beautiful in person than in her picture. And the photo had only hinted at the sensuality that emanated from her and gently reduced him to a mindless state of enthrallment.

That lady was dangerous!

On one level he could readily believe that she was involved in the jewel theft. If so, then she was probably the one who engineered it. Her poor enslaved husband wouldn't have been able to refuse her anything.

But on another level he was ninety-nine percent certain that she was innocent. There was nothing artificial about her. The thick golden hair that was parted in the middle and waved loosely around her face before being caught up in a French twist at her nape had to be natural. That delicate color didn't come from a bottle.

Her face would have been a perfect oval except for a slight squaring at the jaw—possibly an indication of stubbornness? The only makeup she'd worn was a light pink lipstick and maybe dark brown mascara on her long, thick eyelashes. The rosy color just under her high cameolike cheekbones radiated from within. She even seemed unaware of her potent sensuality. Her movements were unaffected and natural.

So where did that leave him?

Confused and disoriented, that's where. Twice he'd almost blown his cover already. The first time when he'd been so conscience stricken by her admiration of his fictitious struggle to get through college that he'd protested instead of basking in her praise as he should have done.

Actually, he'd gotten his degree from U.C., Los Angeles, not from a college in Florida, and in the usual four years. Also, his father had paid most of his expenses while he spent his spare time waterskiing and training for the swim team.

The second mistake was when he'd agreed to take the room without even seeing it. That was dumb. He couldn't very well tell her that he'd been furnished with a copy of the blueprints for the apartment complex and knew where every nook and cranny was.

He'd known before he had ever left Los Angeles that she had no vacancies and he'd have to talk her into renting him the storeroom.

The hotel in downtown Phoenix loomed ahead of him, reminding him of yet another lie. He wasn't staying with friends but had a room on the same floor as the swimming pool and gym in this luxury hotel that gave his firm a generous corporate discount.

When he drove into the valet parking area and stopped, he closed his eyes and lowered his head.

You'd better get it all together, Campbell. Start thinking of this babe as a suspect, not as a desirable woman, because when this is all over, there's no chance in hell that she'll ever forgive you.

Chapter Two

At eight-thirty the following morning Dinah was having a second cup of coffee and going over the mail when Todd showed up on her doorstep dressed in jeans and carrying a duffle bag. There was a happy smile on his face that brought an instant response from her.

"I'm glad you're early," she said as she unlatched the screen door and let him in. "Word's gotten around that we're opening the pool this morning, and the kids are already lining up at the gate, waiting."

Because of the high number of children in the project, the pool area was surrounded by a tall chain-link fence with padlocks on the gates—a requirement of the insurance company.

"I figured they would be," he admitted, "but could you come with me to my room first? I need your help in deciding what pieces of furniture I'll need."

The recreation center was just across one of the narrow streets—called "driveways" within the apartment project—from the manager's apartment where Dinah lived and had her office in the spare bedroom. The large rectangular "rec" building faced the driveway but backed up to the patio, and the windows and sliding glass door in the main room overlooked the entire pool area.

The place was furnished with game tables—pool, Ping-Pong, cards—at the front end and a cozy sitting area at the back where less-active residents could read, visit, or just watch the swimmers. A short hall led to a kitchen on the right, rest rooms on the left, and the storage room at the end.

Dinah unlocked the building and entered with Todd following behind. "We don't open the rec center until after lunch, except on special request," she explained, "so you won't be bothered with people running in and out in the mornings. But don't expect to get any sleep until the place closes at eleven."

"Eleven?" he asked with mock surprise. "I haven't gone to bed before eleven since I left home."

She laughed with him as they walked down the hall, but felt the full weight of the seven years' difference in their ages. She usually went to bed at ten.

After unlocking the door to the storage room, she handed him the key ring. It held three keys, which she identified for him. "This one is for the front door, this one is for your room and the third is for the poolhouse dressing rooms. You'll have to use the showers in there since there are none in the rest rooms."

Todd pocketed them, then eyed her teasingly. "What happens if I get caught going from here to there in the buff?"

She raised her eyebrows and tried to keep a straight face. "If it's a female who catches you she'll probably attack you. When that happens, don't rely on me to come running to your rescue. You can't expect a woman to control her lust if you entice her by traipsing around in the altogether.''

He drew himself up to his full six-foot-one inch height and eyed her with feigned indignation. ''Ms. Swensen! I've spoken to you before about your sexist remarks. If you persist, I'll have to complain to the management about this sexual harassment.''

Dinah shook with suppressed merriment as she poked him in the chest with her finger. ''I *am* the management, buster.''

Their laughter rang through the empty building.

Todd had brought a metal tape measure, and they measured the room and the one window that faced onto the street. It had a pull-down blind but no curtains.

''I'm sorry about the lack of windows,'' she said. ''The room's pretty gloomy without more light, but it wasn't meant to be lived in. The building's air-conditioned so you don't need a breeze, but you'd better get some lamps unless you want to leave the ceiling light on all the time.''

Todd couldn't tell her that the window that looked directly into her living room was the most important reason he'd insisted on renting the room. Instead, he shrugged and said, ''That's okay. I won't be in here during the day so I don't need much in the way of furniture.'' His gaze roamed over the area. ''Mainly a comfortable bed. There's no closet so I'll need a chest with lots of drawers, and...oh, yes...a desk where I can study, plus a couple of chairs.''

''Are you going to have a telephone installed?''

''Oh, sure.'' He'd already arranged for that. The most important piece of equipment an investigator had was his phone. He'd need it to keep in touch with headquarters.

"Mom used to say I was born with a phone growing out of my ear." He chuckled. "And I do remember thinking of it as a sort of umbilical cord. I'll definitely need one."

Dinah looked at her watch. "You've got five minutes before I open the gate," she warned. "I'll get out of here and let you change."

"No need," he said, and before she realized what he was going to do, he'd opened the fly of his jeans and pushed them down, revealing navy blue swim trunks underneath.

Dinah didn't attempt to speak as she fought to regain her composure. For a second she'd thought . . .

She took a deep breath. Good heavens, what was the matter with her? She should have known he'd be wearing his bathing suit under his jeans. Even if he hadn't been, he was just an impetuous kid, and it wasn't as if she'd never seen a nude man. She'd been married for seven years before the divorce. Still, she was relieved that he wore trunks on duty instead of the skimpy bikini that was so popular with young men.

Todd stepped out of his jeans and pulled his knit shirt over his head, then stuffed them in his duffle bag and took her arm. "I'm ready," he quipped. "Shall we confront the mob?"

Todd was an instant hit, and for the rest of the week practically everybody in the complex showed up at the pool, either to swim or just to meet the handsome new lifeguard.

He, on the other hand, checked in with Dinah every morning at eight-thirty to have a cup of coffee with her and to talk over his plans for the day. He met with her again every afternoon at five when he was relieved by a thirty-year-old man who worked as a busboy during the day and for four hours in the evenings and on weekends, moon-lighted as a lifeguard in order to support his family.

At that time Todd supplied the drinks—colas from the dispenser—and gave her an account of how the day had gone. Dinah had never had an employee who was so conscientious before, and she looked forward to their get-togethers.

Although he wore his swim trunks and a loose-fitting shirt in the morning, he always dressed in the afternoon before coming over. On Friday he surprised her by wearing dark slacks and a blue plaid sport shirt instead of his usual jeans and T-shirt, and she couldn't resist commenting. "Todd, you're all dressed up. Do you have a date?"

As soon as the words were out, she was aware of an odd feeling of distaste for that idea.

"I'm not sure yet," he said, handing her one of the ice-cold cans of cola he carried. "I haven't asked her."

"Oh, I wouldn't worry if I were you," she assured him as she walked around the bar that separated the tiny kitchen from the dining room. "I'm sure you don't have any trouble finding girls to go out with you."

His ready smile wasn't quite as cocky as usual as he watched her take two glasses from the cupboard. "That's true, I don't. So will you?"

She waited for him to continue. When he didn't, she prodded as she opened the freezer and put ice in the glasses. "Will I what?"

"Will you go out with me?" There was no levity in his tone. "I'd like to take you to dinner."

Dinah whirled around to look at him, certain that she'd misunderstood. "You want to take *me* out?"

"I'd like very much to take you out, Dinah," he said seriously. "Why are you so surprised? Is it because I work for you?"

Her eyes widened in both disbelief and denial as she shut the freezer door. "Of course it's not because you work here," she said heatedly.

"You're not married, are you?" he asked warily.

"No, not anymore," she answered, then wished she'd just said no and left it at that.

"Is there a special man in your life?"

"No. Please, give me a chance to explain. It's because I'm ... Well, I'm so much older than you."

Todd walked over to where she stood and put the can of cola he held down on the counter. "Oh, how old are you?"

She didn't really want him to know, but now she had to tell him. "I'm thirty-two. I have a baby brother who's only three years younger than you."

He seemed to consider that. "How nice, but what's your age got to do with anything? You do still eat solid food, don't you?" The amusement was back in his eyes.

"Yes, I do," she said waspishly, "and I have my own teeth, too. Darn it all, Todd, you're not taking me seriously. You could have your choice of any of the gorgeous half-naked young women at the pool who keep throwing themselves at you, so why me?"

He reached out and brushed a tendril of hair off her cheek. "You may have your own teeth, but I think your eyesight is going if you can ask a question like that."

He gazed at her tenderly, and his tone was soft. "Don't you ever look in the mirror, lady? I've seen a lot of women in all states of undress, and not one of them comes close to being as beautiful and sexy as you even though I've never seen you less than fully clothed."

He moved his hand to caress her cheek, then cupped her chin and tilted her face up to his. "I'm not looking for a quick lay, Dinah. Right now I just need a friend. Have dinner with me. I've been anticipating it all week."

He'd captured her gaze with those melting brown eyes of his, and she couldn't have refused him anything. "All right," she whispered. "If that's what you want."

He leaned down and kissed the tip of her nose. "That's what I want. Believe it."

Todd chose a popular steak house that offered good food but was hardly romantic. They sat across from each other at the small table and made sure their knees didn't touch as they talked about their jobs.

Dinah had changed from a cotton skirt and blouse—her typical day attire—to a silky multicolored print dress that draped enticingly across the swell of her breasts, and black patent high-heeled pumps that made her legs look even longer and more shapely. Her mass of shimmering blond hair was still done up in the sophisticated twist, and he wondered what it would look like loose and free.

The thought was so enticing that it was all he could do to keep his hands, and his knees, to himself!

He'd wanted to take her to one of the intimate little gourmet places with shadowy booths, candlelight, soft music and good wine, but that would have blown his cover for sure. In that setting he'd never have been able to resist the temptation to take her in his arms and explore those sweet lips. Equally important, no struggling law student paying his way through school working as a lifeguard could afford it!

So they had tenderized steaks, and he felt like a heel as he gently probed her with questions. "Have you always lived in the Phoenix area?" he asked innocently, although he already knew her background from the reports.

She dipped her fork into the steaming baked potato. "No, I was born and raised in St. Paul, Minnesota. My family still lives there."

"Oh? Do you have many brothers and sisters?"

"Just the one brother." There was a wealth of affection in her tone. "Garth is twenty-two and recently graduated from the University of Minnesota."

She smiled at Todd. "You remind me a lot of him. He's about your height, and his hair's only slightly darker than yours, but he wears it longer."

Todd was both pleased and disconcerted—pleased because, since he reminded her of the brother she obviously loved dearly, she'd be more inclined to trust him, and disconcerted because he wanted a lot more from her than sisterly affection.

That unwelcome bit of knowledge brought him up short, and he shut it out as he resumed his subtle interrogation. "Is that where you went to school?" he asked, hoping to lead her on to the subject of her marriage.

She shook her head. "No, I went to UCLA, but I quit after my sophomore year—"

She stopped abruptly, apparently reminded of something she didn't want to discuss. He took a shot in the dark. "Is that when you got married?"

Dinah cringed inwardly as she always did when the subject of her marriage was raised, but she'd known it would be and she dredged up the story she always told.

"Yes," she answered briefly.

She knew that Todd was waiting for her to continue, but she wasn't going to volunteer information. She considered her failed marriage a private and personal matter and no one else's business.

When the silence became uncomfortable, Todd didn't take the hint but prodded gently. "Do you have children?"

"No."

He'd known that, of course, and wondered about it. Didn't she want a family, or had she been unable to conceive? Obviously this wasn't the time to ask her.

"What was your husband like?" he queried instead. "Are you a widow, or—"

"Divorced," she said shortly.

He tried again. "What happened?"

She tried not to be irritated with him. He was only a kid and almost certainly used to openly discussing personal problems with his college pals. Probably she should be flattered that he was interested enough to ask, but that didn't make her any more willing to tell him.

She executed the disinterested shrug she'd perfected for this little bit of playacting. "Not much," she said in a bored tone. "We just weren't compatible. In California it's not necessary to place blame to dissolve a marriage. We were unhappy together so we went our separate ways."

If she hadn't been looking at him she'd have missed the odd expression that flitted across his face. It twisted his features in an unmistakable grimace of pain, almost as though she'd suddenly slapped him, but it was gone so quickly that she decided she must have been mistaken.

When he spoke again, there was an edge of anger to his voice that puzzled her. "Do you still keep in touch with him?"

Apparently there was no end to his questions. It was time to take the initiative and change the subject.

"No," she said, "I haven't heard from him since the dissolution was granted, but I put all that behind me a long time ago so now let's talk about you. Have you ever been married?"

He blinked with surprise but answered promptly. "No. Until now I've never met a woman I wanted to spend the rest of my life with, but when I do I'm sure as hell not going to let her get away.''

Dinah was startled by his vehemence, but couldn't resist a cynical observation. ''Ah, the sweet dreams of youth,'' she observed with a sigh. ''I wish you luck, Todd, and maybe it will happen that way for you, but don't count on it. Love is no longer eternal. It lasts about ten years max. Just take a look at the statistics.''

He was strangely silent after that, leaving it up to her to keep the conversation going. When she tried, he seemed distracted—perhaps moody was a better word—and did little to respond to her attempts. She finally gave up, and they finished the meal in a tense and uncomfortable stillness.

It was still early when they got home, and Dinah wondered whether or not she should invite him in, but he took her key and opened the door for her, then backed away. ''Thanks for going to dinner with me,'' he said politely. ''We'll have to do it again sometime. See you tomorrow.''

He turned and was gone, leaving her gaping after him. He hadn't even given her a chance to thank him for taking her out.

Todd was both furious and hurt. *She lied to me! She looked me right in the eye and deliberately lied to me.*

Viciously he kicked a stone that lay in the middle of the driveway and sent it flying all the way to the end of the block. *We were unhappy together so we went our separate ways.* Ha! She had no intention of telling him that her ex-husband was a thief and in jail and that's why she'd divorced him.

So much for his ninety-nine percent certainty that she wasn't involved in the theft. If she'd lie to him about her divorce then she'd also lie to the police to protect herself and her husband.

As he approached the recreation hall, he could see that it was swarming with people. He'd intended to go to his room, but the only way he could get there was through the crowd, and he was in no mood to be polite. Instead he jammed his hands in his pockets and kept on walking down the road in the dusky twilight, his mind reeling with confused and twisted thoughts.

How could he have been so gullible? He'd always had a natural ability to read people, and the psychology classes he'd taken in college had sharpened that skill. He'd learned to rely on his hunches, but where had he gone so wrong this time?

He muttered an oath and kicked another pebble. Hell, it didn't take many smarts to figure that out. He'd let himself get emotionally involved with her.

Let himself? As he remembered it, he hadn't had any choice in the matter! All she'd had to do was open the door to him that first day and he'd been lost.

Did she affect all men that way, or was it some sort of chemical reaction with him? He wasn't usually distracted by women, at least not when he was investigating them. He was too well trained for that, so what was there about this particular woman that melted his willpower and blinded him to everything but his overwhelming need to find her innocent of any wrongdoing?

There was one inviolate rule for an operative and that was to never become emotionally involved in the case. However, operatives were human like everybody else, and sometimes they broke the rule. There was no disgrace in that as long as they admitted it and asked to be replaced.

Todd knew that's what he should do, was required to do, but damm it, he wasn't going to admit to Wes Nelson that he'd been played for a fool.

He didn't like Wes. The man was a compulsive joker, but his jokes were always put-downs. He rode Todd constantly about being the youngest member of the firm, making stupid remarks like, Does your mother let you stay out after dark? Do you need advice on what to do with a girl when you catch her? Then there had been the constant teasing after they'd been in a bar together one time and the bartender had asked Todd for identification. Wes had seen to it that everyone who worked in the building had known about that.

No, he wasn't going to tell Wes or anyone else that he'd been outsmarted by a blond blue-eyed beauty who looked like Cinderella and lied like Pinocchio. There hadn't been any harm done yet; he'd found her out before he'd done anything to damage the investigation, but from now on he was going to keep his wits about him and check on her all the way.

If she wanted to play games, he was more than willing to accommodate her, and he could play just as dirty as she could.

If only he didn't hurt so bad.

Dinah got out of bed the following morning, lethargic and with a mild headache. She'd been restless all night, twisting and turning while the evening with Todd re-played itself in her mind.

What had she said or done to make him withdraw from her? And even more important, why did it matter so much? She hadn't lost a night's sleep over a male since she'd finally gotten over the shock of Anson's duplicity. She'd vowed then that no man would ever cause her that much grief again, and now here she was fretting over a sulky kid.

The unwelcome memory of Todd's fingers beneath her chin, lifting her face to his, and the touch of his lips on the tip of her nose when he persuaded her to have dinner with him, prompted her to reluctantly acknowledge that this was no adolescent she was dealing with. He may be young, but he was all male and could set even her tattered heart to pounding.

Since it was Saturday and she didn't keep office hours on weekends, she dressed in lilac shorts and a mauve blouse, then ran a brush through her long blond hair and let it swing loose around her shoulders as she padded barefoot to the kitchen. Out of habit she made a full pot of coffee before she remembered that Todd didn't work on weekends, either, and therefore wouldn't be coming over to share it with her.

She wondered how he usually spent his days off. Probably with those pals he'd shared an apartment with before moving in here. Did he have a girlfriend in Phoenix already? He hadn't mentioned one, but Dinah couldn't believe that there weren't several women who would be more than happy to fill the role.

The sharp ring of the telephone interrupted her musing, and for the next several minutes she was busy placating an irate tenant whose air conditioner wasn't cooling properly.

"I'm sorry," she said for at least the third time in the lengthy discourse, "but as I told you, there's no way I can get anyone out to look at it before Monday. The repairmen don't work on weekends, but there are a couple of electric fans in the storeroom you can use until then if you'd care to come and pick them up."

After a few more minutes of grumbling, the tenant finally hung up, and Dinah heaved a sigh. Oh, the joys of being a manager! No matter what went wrong she always got the blame for it. How come nobody ever called to thank her when everything was working right?

She'd just finished pouring the freshly brewed coffee into a thick pottery mug when the doorbell chimed. Oh, no! Now what had broken down? Anxiously she peered out the front kitchen window and was surprised to see Todd standing on her stoop.

Her surprise was replaced with a sudden rush of relief and joy as she hurried to the door and opened it, then unhooked the screen. "Todd," she exclaimed, "I wasn't expecting you this morning. It's your day off."

His smile was as big and sunny as ever, and there was no sign of his peevishness of the night before as he came in and shut the door behind him.

He started to say something, then shut his mouth and just stared at her, his appraisal frank and thorough. "Good Lord, Dinah," he murmured, and there was a puzzling sadness—or was it regret?—mixed with the open admiration on his face. "Why do you hide behind skirts when you've got legs that most women would kill for?"

She felt shy in the heat of his approval, but couldn't resist a teasing smile. "Did you think maybe I had fat thighs?"

He shook his head slowly. "To tell you the honest truth, I sort of hoped you did. Everyone should have at least one flaw."

The teasing smile faded. He wasn't kidding around; he was serious. She'd grown up accustomed to the somewhat lusty admiration of the opposite sex, but she couldn't remember ever having been quite so deeply flattered. Todd really and truly meant what he was saying.

"That's very sweet of you, Todd," she said huskily, unable to find words to tell him how much his compliment really meant to her. "The...the coffee's ready," she finally stammered, changing the subject, "but I...I didn't think you'd stop by this morning. I mean...since you don't have to work today."

Her tongue was tripping all over itself, and she was sure she was repeating things she'd already said. She decided it was time to shut up and let him do the talking.

"I have some plans I need to discuss with you," he said as he followed her into the dining room.

As usual, he didn't sit down immediately but stood until she brought the coffeepot and mugs to the table, then he held her chair before taking a seat beside her. His old-fashioned courtliness never failed to charm her.

Looking at him, she smiled. "Todd, it really isn't necessary for you to stand every time I come into the room, but I'd like you to know that it's a most endearing trait. I realize that the women's organizations discourage that sort of thing as condescending, but it makes me feel very, very special."

His gaze softened and he reached out and put his hand over hers where it lay on the table. "You are very, very special," he murmured tenderly, but then, almost as if he regretted the remark, he pulled his hand back and grinned. "I have a mother who insisted that I mind the manners she spent so much time teaching me. It's just second nature with me now."

Dinah felt a little put down but was determined not to show it. "Do your parents live in Florida?" she asked, hoping to learn more about his background.

"Uh...yes," he answered, hesitating as though he wasn't sure.

"Do you have brothers and sisters?"

"Yeah. One brother, twenty, and two sisters, one sixteen and the little one is nine."

"That's quite a range in age," Dinah observed. "Your mother must be fairly young."

He nodded. "She's forty-five and looks thirty-five." There was a note of pride in his tone. "People are always mistaking her for my older sister."

Dinah winced, and the coffee in her mug sloshed. No wonder he was attracted to her. She probably reminded him of his mother!

She was thankful when he changed the subject. "I want to sound you out about some projects I have in mind," he said, suddenly all business. "I'd like to start up some swimming classes. I understand it's been some time since the last ones were offered."

"Yes, it has been," she admitted. "Our last full-time lifeguard didn't like to teach, and the part-time ones don't consider it their job. I'm delighted that you're willing to do it. When did you want to start?"

"I'd like to put up notices in the rec hall today and begin classes Monday morning. I'll take beginners first, but when we get those going, I'd also like to set up advanced sessions and include lifesaving. Also, I think everyone who uses the pool should be required to attend at least one class in water safety no matter how well they swim."

"That's a great idea," she said enthusiastically, "but I have to warn you that I can't pay you extra for those duties. It's just not in the budget."

He shrugged. "No need. It's all part of the job description. I hope you'll sit in on the first few sessions, and of course you'll be expected to attend the class in water safety like everyone else." He looked at her curiously. "You do swim, don't you?"

She laughed. "Yes, but I have to admit that I'm more of a paddler than a swimmer. I don't have time for lazing around the pool during the day, and besides, it's always jam-packed with rowdy kids. If I go in at all, it's after it's closed for the night."

Todd's expression telegraphed his disapproval. "You should never swim alone when there's nobody around. It's dangerous," he said grimly. "I want you to promise that when you get the urge to go in the pool at night, you'll come and get me. I'd enjoy swimming with you, but I most certainly wouldn't enjoy worrying about you."

She was puzzled by his concern. "But that's not necessary. I may not be an excellent swimmer but I'm competent, and I'm certainly old enough to take responsibility for my own well-being."

"I don't give a damn how old you are," he stated angrily. "Now promise that you'll stay out of the pool in the middle of the night."

She threw him a startled look and stiffened. "Todd!" Her tone was laced with resentment. "I don't have to promise you anything."

He pushed back his chair and jumped up so vigorously that he nearly knocked it over. Jamming his hands in his pockets, he stood with his back to her as an agonizing silence shimmered between them.

Dinah's resentment evaporated and was replaced by shame. He was only trying to protect her; why had she snapped at him? Six years ago she'd have given anything if Anson had shown a fraction of the concern for her that Todd had just displayed. She'd grown up since then, and her independence had been hard won, but that was no excuse for overreacting to Todd's reasonable request.

She got up and walked over to him and put her hand on the back of his shoulder. The muscles beneath his thin shirt twitched.

"I'm sorry." Her voice was whispery with emotion. "You're right. It's stupid to swim at night with no one around."

She leaned her forehead against his back. "I appreciate your caring."

With a little groan he turned and put his arms around her. "Oh, I care," he murmured, and rubbed his cheek in her hair. "But that's no excuse for my temper tantrum. I'm the one who's behaving badly, not you. Can you forgive me?"

Forgive him? The moment he took her in his arms, she forgot everything but the feel of his body against hers, the fresh sea fragrance of his shaving lotion, and the texture of his skin as she snuggled her face against the side of his neck.

She hardly remembered what she was supposed to forgive him for but knew she'd condone anything he wanted if he'd just continue to hold her.

"I promise not to go in the pool unless you're there," she whispered against his ear, and cuddled into his embrace.

For several minutes they just stood there holding each other until she realized that Todd was trembling. She raised her head and brushed his cheek with hers. "Are you all right?" she asked, and recognized the desire that vibrated in her tone.

"No, I'm not," he answered tremulously. "I'd better leave, right now."

His arms tightened around her for a moment, but then he let her go, and without another word left the apartment, shutting the door behind him.

Chapter Three

The first swimming class began at nine o'clock on Monday morning and was a splashing success. The area was swarming with children when Dinah and Todd went down to open the gates, and the two of them had to make some quick changes in their plans.

Dinah knew for sure that most of the older kids had already taken beginner classes, but Todd didn't want to turn anyone away, so he decided to start the advanced classes immediately instead of waiting. It took most of the time he'd set aside just to register the students and collect the parental consent slips, but he announced that as of the following day the beginners would start at eight-thirty followed immediately by the advanced.

That abolished Dinah and Todd's early-morning coffee klatches, and for the rest of the week Dinah was tied up in the afternoons with business meetings and assorted problems at the other properties she managed. Although she sat in on his classes the first couple of days as he'd requested, she didn't see him alone again until Friday when she went to the pool area to speak with a tenant.

She'd finished her conversation and turned to leave when he called to her. Turning back, she saw him hurrying toward her, and again was struck by the graceful symmetry of his nearly nude body. The tight-fitting swimsuit he wore today accentuated his maleness. The man was gorgeous! There was no other way to describe him, and her body's reaction reminded her she was female in every sense of the word.

"Hey, Dinah, wait up." He sprinted across the wet tiles and stopped in front of her. "How about having dinner with me again tonight? We haven't had a chance to talk all week."

Her disappointment was sharp and irrational, but she tried not to let it show. "Oh, I'm sorry, Todd, but I already have a date."

He looked startled. "You have?"

She couldn't help but laugh, although she wasn't sure whether to be flattered or insulted. "Yes, I have. Does that surprise you?"

"Yes. I mean, no, of course it doesn't surprise me. I'm just disappointed. Who's the lucky fellow?"

Her amusement faded. There were times when Todd's brash inquisitiveness was a little jarring. "A friend of mine. You wouldn't know him."

She started to walk away, but he caught her arm. "Wait a minute. Don't be in such a hurry," he said. "Are you free tomorrow?"

Dinah knew she should tell him no. She had no business encouraging his puzzling interest in her. It would be disastrous for her to become emotionally involved with Todd Campbell. She was too old for him—not only in years but in experience. She had a past he didn't know about, a notorious one that she'd run away from five years ago. One she'd hesitate to involve any man in, but especially a clean-cut, idealistic young law student.

She opened her mouth to dismiss him with a refusal, but the words wouldn't come. She wanted to be alone with him again, and he was right, they did have to talk. She needed a report on how the swim classes were going and what he had planned in the way of activities for the rest of the summer. This was part of Dinah's duties as manager, and if he was willing to give it to her on his day off, the least she could do was cooperate.

"Yes, I'm free tomorrow," she admitted.

His bright smile reappeared. "Good, then spend it with me. We'll go to Sedona if that's okay with you. I've heard a lot about it, and it sounds like a great treat for a newcomer like me. We'll have plenty of time to talk business and have fun, too. You do like art galleries and spectacular scenery, don't you?" he added teasingly.

Sedona was a small city approximately one hundred miles north of Phoenix at the southern end of Oak Creek Canyon, which served as a starting point for scenic drives through the rugged Red Rocks area. It was also a picturesque center for contemporary and traditional arts—a "must see" for tourists and residents alike.

Dinah was sorely tempted. She'd only been to Sedona once and had always intended to go back, but somehow had never found the time. Oh, why not? She was entitled to enjoy herself once in a while, and Todd needed a guide.

"I love art galleries and spectacular scenery," she said with a happy smile, "and I can't think of a nicer way to spend my day off, either. I'll fix breakfast before we leave. How do you like your eggs?"

Todd spent the rest of the afternoon vacillating between euphoria and despair. Tomorrow he was going to spend the whole day with Dinah, and he couldn't remember ever being so excited about a date. On the other hand this was no mating dance, and he'd damn well better not forget it. This was a fishing expedition. He intended to find out all he could about Dinah Swensen Erhardt's relationship with her ex-husband.

Now that he'd had time to think it over, he realized that he'd overreacted to her version of the reasons for her divorce. She hadn't actually lied to him; she just had not told him the whole truth.

He'd been a jerk to expect her to bare such a sordid story to a man she hardly knew. It didn't mean she was in on the theft, just that she wasn't going to parade her private anguish for all to see.

Besides, who was he to accuse her of lying when he'd practically done nothing but lie ever since she'd opened the door to him the first time? He'd lied to her about his schooling, his occupation, his reason for being in Phoenix.

As for being evasive, he was an expert at that. He hadn't mentioned that his P.I. firm had arranged for her other lifeguard's offer of a better job in order to create a vacancy for Todd to fill.

Hell, compared to him, she was a saint!

For the first time since becoming a private investigator, he felt revulsion for the duplicity the job demanded. He'd told Wes Nelson that he wouldn't seduce any woman in order to get information, and he wouldn't. But it was even worse to make love to Dinah because he wanted her so badly he couldn't help himself, then go ahead and get the information anyway.

If he found that he couldn't keep his burgeoning feelings under control, he'd have to ask to be taken off the case, and that could well be career suicide.

Then there was the other thing that bothered him. Who was the guy Dinah was going out with tonight?

A twist of something that felt a lot like jealousy knotted his stomach. She'd told him she wasn't involved with a man, and the reports his firm had received confirmed that, so where did this fellow come from?

A dark thought tightened the knot in his gut. Was he someone she was seeing secretly? Maybe someone carrying covert messages between her and her ex-husband?

The very idea was repugnant, but he had to know. The time had come for him to get down to the serious business of this stakeout!

When Todd got off work, he showered and pulled on cutoffs and a T-shirt, then went to his room where he dug his high-powered camera out of his locked suitcase and attached the telescopic lens. He set it on top of the three-drawer chest he'd bought specifically to fit between the now-curtained window and the wall and hold his investigative equipment as well as his clothes.

Pulling open the top drawer, he retrieved his binoculars from underneath his clean briefs and T-shirts, and adjusted the focus so he could see every detail of the front of Dinah's apartment. Briefly, he considered setting up the telescope on the tripod, but dismissed it. Once assembled, it was too large to hide, and too difficult to explain in case someone came into the room and saw it. He'd save that until he needed to see through the windows and into the apartment.

The very idea of spying on Dinah like that made him sick.

Dinah slid the lime-green dress over her head and zipped it up in the back. She loved to dress up, and dinner at an upscale restaurant with an old and dear friend gave her the opportunity.

She hadn't seen Bernie Rose since she'd left Los Angeles five years ago, and she wanted to look nice for him. He and his wife, Sarah, had been the closest friends she and Anson had had during their marriage, and they were the only ones who publicly supported her during those hellish months leading up to, and during, the trial....

Quickly she tuned out that thought, but her hands shook as she brushed her hair up and wrapped it in a loose bun on top of her head, then anchored it with the two jeweled combs she'd inherited years ago from her grandmother.

As she walked back into the living room, she heard a car drive up in front of the apartment. She opened the door and ran out to greet the good-looking, dark-haired man who was coming up the walk.

"Bernie!" she cried, and threw herself into his outstretched arms. "Oh, Bernie, it's so good to see you."

They stood in the middle of the walkway, hugging, and her eyes were blurred with tears when they finally pushed apart to look at each other.

"Dinah!" he exclaimed. "You're just as beautiful as ever. How are you?"

They continued up the walk, each with an arm around the other's waist, and once they were inside, he held her away and looked at her again. "I was wrong," he said. "You're even more beautiful than before. There's an air of maturity about you that's most becoming."

Her gaze also traveled over him. "You're looking good, too, Bernie, but don't try to kid me that everything's all right with you again. You can't hide your pain from me—" Her voice broke, and she swallowed. "Oh, Bernie, I'm so sorry about Sarah...."

She was in his arms once more, and both of them were crying. "I know you are, honey." His tone betrayed his grief. "Losing her was hell, but watching her die was even worse. That awful disease . . . Toward the end I prayed for her to be released from her suffering."

For a few minutes they held each other as they fought to regain their composure. Finally Dinah spoke again. "I would have come. I wanted to . . ."

He wiped at his wet eyes with the back of his hand. "I never doubted that, but at the time you were fighting your own demons here. I meant it when I told you to stay away. Sarah wouldn't have known you, and coming back to Los Angeles would only have made your own struggle harder."

He released her then and stepped back. Taking a handkerchief from his pocket, he handed it to her and smiled. "Blow your nose and wipe your eyes, and then let's put all that behind us. We have a lot of catching up to do, so why don't you fix us each a drink while I go wash my face? Our dinner reservations aren't until seven-thirty."

They relaxed over drinks and light conversation for half an hour, then left the apartment to go to dinner. Bernie had just opened the car door and started to help her in when a voice called to her. "Dinah, wait a minute. I've got a problem."

She recognized Todd's voice and straightened to see him hurrying across the driveway toward them.

"Hey, I'm sorry," he said, then looked at Bernie and stuck out his hand with a wide, boyish grin. "Hi, I'm Todd Campbell, the new lifeguard." His tone was young and friendly.

Bernie smiled and took the proffered hand. "Glad to meet you. I'm Bernard Rose. Is there something we can do for you?"

Dinah was puzzled. Todd certainly looked and sounded cordial enough, but she was picking up vibes from him that were anything but. It disturbed her that she was so sensitive to his displeasure, but no matter how well he hid it, she knew he was upset.

When he answered the question, he was apologetic. "Yeah, there is, but I didn't mean to catch you just as you were going out." He turned his attention to Dinah. "I seem to have misplaced the key to my room, and I'm going out this evening. Could I borrow an extra one until tomorrow? If I don't find mine by then, I'll have another one made."

She wondered what his real problem was but wasn't going to make an issue of it. "Of course. I'll get one for you." She turned and walked back to her apartment.

When Dinah went inside, Todd looked at her escort. "She's a real nice lady to work for," he said innocently. "Have you known her long, Mr. Rose?"

"Bernie," the other man said easily. "Yeah, I've known her for years. What's the matter, kid, you got a crush on her?" He sounded jovial, but there was no amusement in his eyes.

Todd hadn't expected that question, but he hoped his confusion would be mistaken for embarrassment. "Well, yeah, I guess I have," he said shyly. "What man wouldn't?"

There were times when Todd's ability to look younger than his years came in handy, and this appeared to be one of them. Bernie relaxed and grinned. "What man, indeed," he agreed. "Just don't let it get out of control."

Todd bristled, but struggled to hide his anger. "You're probably right," he said, striving to sound naive and agreeable. "Besides, I have my hands full fending off all those teenage girls who come to the pool to seduce the lifeguard. Do you work in property management, too?''

Bernie laughed. "Me? Hell, no, I own a car dealership in Pasadena. I'm just passing through Phoenix on my way to Detroit on business, and stopped to see . . ."

Their conversation was interrupted when Dinah came back with the key. "Here you are, Todd," she said, handing it to him, "but be careful not to lose this one, too. We can't have keys lying around for anyone who finds them to pick up."

His was on his key ring right where it belonged, but he tried to look contrite as he apologized, then waved good-bye as they drove off.

So Bernard Rose was from the Los Angeles area and had known Dinah for years. That probably meant that he'd known her husband, too. What did he really want? and why had Dinah greeted him like a long-lost lover?

What was going on between her and this . . . this car dealer?

The French restaurant where Bernie took Dinah was elegant. They lingered over the six courses, and talked about what had been happening in their lives since they'd last seen each other.

Neither of them mentioned Anson Erhardt, and Dinah hoped they could continue to avoid bringing him into the conversation. She didn't want to talk about her ex-husband. Even though he'd admitted his guilt to her once he'd been indicted, she'd stood by him during the trial and refused to testify against him, knowing all the while that when it was over she'd file for divorce no matter what the outcome.

It had taken her a long time to get over the shock and grief, but she'd finally worked her way through it. Now she felt nothing for Anson—neither contempt nor sympathy. He'd become a nonperson to her, and she wanted to keep it that way.

It was after eleven when they got back to Dinah's apartment, but Bernie seemed reluctant to end the evening. "I have something for you," he said as he parked his shiny new Town Car at the curb. "Do you mind if I come in for a while?"

Normally she didn't invite her dates in at this hour of the night, but Bernie was the widower of her best friend. "Please do," she said. "I'll make coffee. I'm not used to a different wine with every course, and I could use a little sobering up."

They both chuckled, and Bernie reached across her to unlock the glove compartment and take out a beautifully wrapped package. He carried it in one hand and put his other arm around her waist as they walked to the front door.

In the living room he placed it on the coffee table. "Why don't you get the coffee started before you open it?"

It wasn't like Bernie to give her a gift. The two couples had always exchanged birthday, anniversary and Christmas presents during the good times, but it had been Dinah and Sarah who remembered the dates and selected the articles. She was pleased but also a little uneasy. A gift could have so many different connotations.

When Dinah had finished in the kitchen, she returned to the living room and picked up the package. "Now can I open it?" she asked, excitement giving a lilt to her voice as she began removing the ribbon.

Bernie chuckled. "Go ahead. You always did get as excited as a kid over a present."

She put the ribbon and bow down, then ripped off the colorful paper to expose a square white box. After opening the lid, she removed an object wrapped in several layers of tissue paper.

"Bernie, you clown," she said as she peeled the soft wrapping away. "If you've given me a box full of paper I'll..." She caught her breath as the last covering drifted to the floor. "Oh, Bernie, it's Sarah's egg!"

It was indeed Sarah Rose's enamel, gold-encrusted Fabergé egg, not one of the fifty-odd fabled imperial Easter eggs created by Peter Carl Fabergé for the last two Russian czars, but a treasure nevertheless. Sarah's egg had been made for her Russian great-great-grandmother by an admirer, one of the young artists who worked in the Fabergé workshops in St. Petersburg during the middle of the nineteenth century.

Although it was not executed by the immortal master jeweler, it was a rare bootleg copy of one of his designs. This one had no jewels, but was liberally decorated with gold and had been Sarah's most cherished heirloom.

Dinah's hands shook as she set the delicate piece on the table. "Bernie, I can't accept that." Her tone was tremulous. "It belongs to Sarah's family."

Bernie shook his head sadly. "Sarah has no family left but me, and I'm too clumsy to handle something like that. I don't want to be responsible for it."

He put his arm around her and hugged her against him. "Take it, honey. She'd want you to have it."

Again Dinah's eyes filled with tears. "All right, if you're sure," she murmured. "But I wish she were still here to enjoy it herself."

When the coffee was finished, Dinah fixed a tray and took it into the living room where Bernie was sitting on the sofa. She set it on the low table and filled the cups, then passed one to Bernie along with a crystal plate of his favorite peanut butter cookies, which she'd baked earlier in the day.

"I knew there was a reason why I was so eager to see you," he said with a grin as he took several of the goodies and placed them on a napkin. "You always did cater to my cookie addiction."

She sat down beside him with her own cup. "It was Anson's cookie addiction I catered to," she said lightly. "You just always showed up on baking day."

As soon as she'd finished the sentence, she knew it had been a mistake. She hadn't intended to mention her husband, and now that she had, it gave Bernie the opening he'd apparently been waiting for.

"Do you ever hear from him, Dinah?" he asked softly.

As always, when Anson was mentioned she drew into herself, not wanting to feel the humiliation and pain that was always there beneath the surface, waiting to be recalled.

"No." Her tone was crisp. "He doesn't know where I am. At least I've never told him. I haven't had any contact with him since the trial."

"Sarah and I visited him a couple of times before she got so sick," Bernie said cautiously. "We...we just wanted to make sure he was...you know...all right." He sounded apologetic. "I mean...well, hell, he'd been like a brother to me...."

His voice trailed off as she wrapped her arms around her waist and leaned forward, trying to ward off the words that ripped open healing wounds deep inside her.

"I don't want to hear it!" she cried in desperation. "For six years I was happy being his wife. I loved him, and he said he loved me. We were getting along well financially, so why did he do such an awful thing?"

Her voice had risen, but she couldn't lower it. "How could he put our whole future in jeopardy with such an insane—"

"He says he didn't take those gems, Dinah," Bernie interrupted, "and they were never found. Is there some reason why you don't believe him? Do you know something the police don't?"

She was appalled. This conversation was out of hand. She'd already said far too much.

She straightened and stood up. "Please don't make me live that all over again, Bernie. It's still too painful—"

He stood, too, immediately contrite. "Oh, hey, honey, I'm sorry," he said, and put his hands on her shoulders. "I didn't mean to upset you."

She moved away from him, and made an effort to get control of herself. "I'm sorry, too," she said. "It's my fault. I should have warned you that I don't like to talk about the past. I've made a whole new life for myself here in Arizona and I'm content. What happened between Anson and me is personal and private. It's also over. I don't look back anymore, only ahead."

"Of course," Bernie said apologetically. "I didn't mean to pry." He glanced at his watch. "It's time for me to leave, but before I go, there's something I feel you should know. It's probably not been mentioned in the newspapers out here, but the ones in California have a renewed interest in the case."

Dinah stared at him, unable to guess what he was leading up to. He quickly filled her in.

"Anson Erhardt is coming up for parole in a couple of weeks. The word is that he's been a model prisoner so he'll probably be released."

* * *

Todd arrived promptly at seven the following morning. Dinah greeted him in a bright blue sundress. "Hi," she said cheerfully. "Breakfast's ready to be put on the table, so if you'll just sit down we can eat before everything gets cold."

He grinned and picked up the coffee carafe from the counter. "I'll pour while you serve, but we don't need to hurry. We have all day. For that matter I'm free all weekend if you'd like to prolong the trip and maybe run on up to the Grand Canyon."

Her eyes widened, and he quickly backed off. "That's not a proposition. We could stay in separate cabins. I just thought that as long as we were that close we could—"

"That's out of the question," Dinah said firmly. "I have other plans for tomorrow."

What was Todd up to? More important, what did he want of her?

Dinah hadn't had much experience with men. She'd dated teenage boys in high school, and there was never any doubt about what they wanted. She'd quickly established the fact that she didn't sleep around, and, although it hadn't stopped them from trying, it had been more of a game than a serious seduction.

She'd met Anson Erhardt, who was twenty-two and a senior, within days after she started at UCLA, and dated him steadily until they were married two years later. He was the only man she'd ever made love with, and since their traumatic divorce she'd remained aloof from any kind of involvement other than casual friendships.

Todd Campbell puzzled her. It didn't make sense that he'd pass up all the sexy young sea nymphs who swarmed around him every day in favor of a disillusioned divorcée in her thirties. She knew she had the kind of looks that appealed to the opposite sex. She'd have to be deaf not to since they'd been telling her so since she was twelve years old, but she'd never had one so much younger pursue her.

Maybe it was her fault. She couldn't deny that she responded to his attention. He made her heart speed up and all her senses come alive every time they were together, and she hadn't had any luck at hiding it from him. That day just a week ago when he'd held her in his arms she'd practically melted.

But what bewildered her most was that it had been Todd who walked away from that encounter. She knew he'd been affected. She couldn't have been that intimately entwined with him and not know, but still he hadn't even tried to take it any further. Instead he'd almost dashed out of the house and hadn't referred to the episode since.

Now he was suggesting they spend the weekend together but in separate cabins even though the sexual tension between them was almost combustible.

She might not know much about men, but she knew that was definitely not the usual reaction of a twenty-five-year-old male.

An hour later Todd and Dinah were on Highway 17, in Todd's beat-up old Thunderbird, leaving the metropolitan area behind. She'd offered her newer Toyota, but he'd declined.

"We can take the Corolla if you'd feel more comfortable," he'd said, "but don't sell this baby of mine short. She may look like a wreck, but her engine purrs like a kitten, and I guarantee she'll get us there and back with no problem."

Dinah could see that he preferred to drive his own car, so she hid her misgivings and agreed. Now she had to admit that he'd been right; it ran smoothly and quietly. Obviously he'd done a lot of work on it.

They both relaxed after they got through the metropolitan traffic and traveled north on the flat plains that were actually ancient valleys that had been filled in by rocks and soil washed down from the mountains. The dry desert heat wasn't too uncomfortable, and they left their windows down to enjoy the fresh, clean air uncontaminated by the pollutants of the city.

Dinah breathed deeply and sighed. "Mmm, it's good to get away from all the people, and the cars and the problems. I'd forgotten how sparsely populated rural Arizona is."

Todd agreed. "I think it's great. It's getting harder to find wide-open space anymore."

He reached over and took her hand. "You look bright-eyed and happy this morning." His gaze roamed over her briefly before turning back to the road. "Do you know that you have the sexiest hair I've ever seen? You should wear it down all the time."

She squeezed his hand in thanks. "That's very sweet of you, but I don't wear shorts or let my hair hang down my back when I'm working. It's unprofessional. I'm the apartment manager, not the resident sexpot."

She grinned impishly. "However, nights and weekends I'm free to be as uninhibited as I want."

He chuckled and nestled her hand against his thigh. "Watch it, love, or I'll renew my invitation to spend the weekend together but withdraw the offer of separate cabins."

They both laughed, but then he sobered. "Did you have a good time with Mr. Rose last night?" His tone was casual, but she felt the sudden tightening of the muscles in his hand and leg.

"Yes, it was very nice," she said, and wished he hadn't brought up the subject.

She hadn't known that Anson was eligible for parole, and it affected her more than she wanted to admit. She was glad that he wouldn't have to serve any more time in prison. His crime, after all, hadn't been one of violence, but still his probable release made her uneasy.

He hadn't wanted the divorce. She'd filed for it anyway, but surely he wouldn't try to find her. It wouldn't be hard; she hadn't made much of an effort to hide. There was no need.

It wasn't that she was afraid of him. Anson had always seemed like a gentle person, although obviously she hadn't known him nearly as well as she'd thought she had. It had taken her a long time to get over his deceit, and she didn't want him coming back into her life no matter how briefly.

"Are you going out with him again tomorrow?" Todd asked, breaking into her thoughts.

She blinked. "Bernie? No. Why?"

The muscles in his hand and arm relaxed, and he shrugged. "No reason. You said you couldn't spend the weekend with me because you had other plans, so I just assumed..."

"You assumed wrong," she said primly. "Bernie left early this morning for Detroit."

Todd was relieved to hear that. He didn't know how the mysterious Bernard Rose figured in Dinah's past, but he intended to find out. He'd taken pictures of him with his telephoto lens when Bernie had arrived at her apartment yesterday, then had had them developed at a one-hour place and had faxed them to the office in L.A. along with the man's name and occupation.

He'd instructed Wes to find out everything he could about Rose and hoped to have the information Monday—Tuesday at the latest.

Chapter Four

At Cordes Junction the highway veered northeast and into the green rolling terrain of Coconino National Forest. Approximately thirty miles south of Sedona, Todd and Dinah stopped at Montezuma Castle National Monument, the ruins of a prehistoric cliff dwelling.

Dinah had been there before, but Todd had never seen anything like it and he was fascinated. "I read about the cliff dwellings in school," he said as they walked along the Sycamore Trail and gazed at the shallow cave near the top of a limestone cliff high above them. It was honeycombed with five stories of small oblong rooms. "It was interesting enough, but to actually see them still standing after seven or eight hundred years is mind-boggling. I just wish there were some way we could go inside."

Dinah shook her head regretfully. "So do I, but the foundation is almost fifty feet high, and the rooms were inaccessible except by ladders. The monument would be defaced and eventually destroyed if steps were built and the public allowed to scramble through them."

Later, the approach to Sedona in the heart of the Red Rock country was a spectacular visual treat. The sweeping curves of the road cut through sagebrush country brightened with sycamore-lined washes, until ahead of them was their first view of the town. Built on gently sloping hills, it was surrounded by a forest of evergreen trees with a backdrop of high, erosion-carved red and gold buttes.

"I never knew Arizona was so beautiful," Todd said, his tone hushed with wonder. "I thought it was all desert and Indian reservations."

"A lot of people have that impression," Dinah assured him. "They don't realize that with irrigation even our deserts and barren plateaus can be made productive."

By the time they reached the village of Tlaquepaque, a Spanish-style arts-and-crafts complex within the town of Sedona, it was one o'clock. Their first stop was at one of the small restaurants in the charming setting of white stucco buildings with red tile roofs, open arches and tiled walkways.

They were given a window table where they could look out on the courtyards decorated with colorful potted plants, fountains and a statuary. Graceful old sycamore trees had been retained, and their trunks writhed through passageways created for them by the architects.

"I suppose you're going to want to browse through every boutique and gallery in here," Todd groused good-naturedly as he bit into his three-decker club sandwich.

She swallowed a mouthful of fruit salad before answering. "Darn tootin'. I'm going to try on all the clothes, examine every painting and run my hands over every statuette. This is an artist's paradise. A couple of years ago one of the magazines polled its readers on their favorite place in America to shop for art, and Sedona placed sixth on the list. Even ahead of New York."

"I'm not surprised," Todd said. "If I can manage to lure you away from your shopping in time, I'd like to take the scenic drive through Oak Creek Canyon."

"Oh, I'm not going to shop," she told him regretfully. "I left my bank credit card at home. I knew I couldn't trust my good sense in the midst of all this temptation. I'm just going to look and touch."

"Women." Todd sighed in mock disgust. "If you want to look at and touch something, I'm available. You don't have to seek out an inanimate object. I guarantee you I'd appreciate it a hell of a lot more than a statue would, too."

Dinah wished he wouldn't tease her like that. Doing so ignited a longing in her to comply with his request. She found it hard to ignore even though she knew he was just kidding.

This time she didn't ignore it but reached across the small table and put her hand over his. "Poor baby," she crooned in exaggerated sympathy. "Haven't you been getting your strokes lately?"

He turned his hand over and grasped hers tightly. "I haven't been getting any strokes from you at all and you know it." His voice was tight with frustration. "It drives me crazy to listen to you talk about wanting to caress a cold bronze figure when I'd sell my soul to feel your soft little hands touching and rubbing and patting my warm flesh."

His words and his anguished tone sent a wave of desire flooding through her that left her mute and unable to think, let alone speak. She could only stare and hope her face didn't reflect her yearning.

For a few moments the silence between them was charged with raw sensuality, then Todd pushed back his chair and stood up. "Excuse me," he muttered hoarsely, "I'll be back in a minute," and walked outside.

Dinah clasped her hands together and took a deep breath. She was stunned by the strength of her wanton need for Todd Campbell. If they'd been alone in a private place instead of in a public restaurant, she'd be in his arms now, caressing him in all the ways he wanted her to, in all the places she wanted to touch, and there'd be no stopping them.

She took another deep breath, then reached for her glass of ice water and held the cold wet surface to her temple. Obviously it had been too long since she'd been with a man. She knew she had a passionate nature. Her years of marriage had taught her that, but she'd thought Anson had killed her passion as well as her love when she found out how greedy and unprincipled he was.

On the other hand if it was just sex she needed, why did it have to be Todd she lusted after? She'd dated a lot of men in the past five years, and all of them had tried to seduce her. Although she was sorry that her unresponsiveness frustrated them, she'd never felt a need to relieve their frustration.

None of them had ever aroused her the way Todd did, and he was the only one that was totally unsuitable for a lover.

Maybe that was it—the old "forbidden fruit" allure. He was too young, not only in age but in maturity and worldliness. That put him off-limits and therefore made him all the more desirable.

After a few minutes Todd returned, acting endearingly embarrassed. "I'm sorry," he said, not quite looking at her as he slid into his seat across from her. "I guess I made a real fool of myself."

She hadn't yet conquered the urge to reach out and touch him, but she kept her hands firmly on her own side of the table. "Not at all, Todd," she said huskily. "I . . . I didn't realize I'd been leading you to believe—"

"You haven't," he interrupted. "It's not your fault that you're so appealing. I just sort of got carried away. It won't happen again." He picked up his sandwich and started to eat.

The next two hours were spent exploring the boutiques and galleries of the quaint village, and gradually the awkwardness between them dissolved as they tried on designer hats, hand-painted scarves and exquisitely tooled leather belts. Todd bought Dinah a pair of large dangling enameled earrings in the radiant color of the buttes, and she bought him a handcrafted leather wallet with his initials hastily worked into the design.

Shortly after four o'clock they decided to leave the rest of Tlaquepaque's enticing shops for perhaps another trip at a later date and headed for Oak Creek Canyon.

Their first stop was at Chapel of the Holy Cross, an inverted wedge of concrete aggregate and glass designed to blend in perfect harmony with the jagged red rock cliffs on which it was perched. The only ornamentation was a ninety-foot-high cross bisecting the south face.

"I understand the church was commissioned by a local sculptor as a memorial to her parents," Dinah told Todd.

"What a magnificent way to honor the memory of someone you love," he said.

A short way from there they spotted the huge and colorful sentinels of Cathedral Rock, one of the most striking landmarks of the area. Todd pulled over and parked so they could get out of the car and look at it. "I recognize that," he said. "My parents used to have a calendar with that scene on it."

"Yes, it's a favorite on calendars all over the world," she answered dreamily. "Anson and I had a beautiful one that was given out one year by the shop where he worked."

"Was Anson your husband?"

Todd's question was asked so offhandedly that she answered "yes" before she realized she'd mentioned her ex-husband's name.

The next question was equally casual. "What kind of work did he do?"

"He was a gemologist," she said with what she hoped was equal casualness, then turned and started walking around the car toward the passenger side as she firmly changed the subject. "We'd better not tarry too long if we want to see all the sights."

As they drove north, the canyon rose, narrowed and gradually changed character, becoming cool and densely wooded. Vertical rock walls with an occasional ponderosa pine growing out of them gave way to steep slopes of dark pine forest.

"I'll bet there are trout in that creek," said Todd referring to the clear, rocky stream at the side of the road.

She glanced at him. "Do you like to fish?"

"Love to," he answered wistfully. "Especially fly-fishing in a fast-moving mountain stream. There's nothing like it. I even tie my own flies."

"Then you'll have to come up here on weekends. Fishing is one of the main attractions, and there are lots of campgrounds."

"If I do, will you come with me?" he asked, never taking his eyes off the road. "You can have your own tent and sleeping bag," he hastened to assure her.

Just the thought of spending a weekend with Todd in this magnificent setting made her shiver, and she knew that the last thing she'd want would be her own tent and sleeping bag.

"I . . . I don't know, Todd." She sounded breathless. "I don't think that's a good idea."

He reached over and took her hand. "I think it's a wonderful idea," he said huskily. "I promise that I can be a gentleman when I put my mind to it."

She squeezed his hand. "You're always a gentleman, but I'm not immune to you, you know. In fact, if you want the honest truth, I'm not sure I could resist you if we spent a weekend alone together. That's why I'm hesitant. Just because I'm a divorcée doesn't mean I sleep around."

He opened his mouth to protest, but she hurried on. "I was married very young, and my husband is the only lover I've ever had."

Todd looked so disbelieving that she had to laugh. "Oh, come on now, monogamy isn't all that unusual."

"But you've been divorced for years. Surely there have been others since then."

Dinah wondered when celibacy had become a sin. "No, there hasn't. Our divorce was a devastating one, and since then I haven't met a man I wanted to be that intimate with."

Todd had slowed almost to a stop as he watched her while she spoke. "Including me?" he asked quietly.

She was silent for a moment, trying to find the right words. "No, not including you," she finally admitted. "You're the first one who's seriously tempted me, but you're also the first one that I couldn't possibly have a summer fling with."

"A *fling*," he said with amusement.

"Oh, all right," she snapped. "You probably have a different word for it now, but that's what we called it when I was in school."

Todd was still holding her hand, but now he grasped her at the wrist as he pulled over and stopped the car. "That's what this is all about, isn't it?" he grated. "The difference in our ages. Why does that bug you so? Am I so clumsy and immature that you're ashamed to be with me?"

"Of course not," she scoffed, "and you're far too self-confident to believe that for a minute. Why are you doing this to me, Todd? I've tried every way I know to discourage your attentions, so why won't you leave me alone?"

That wasn't true and she knew it. If she'd really wanted to discourage him, she could have done it easily; she'd had plenty of experience discouraging other men. Instead she'd played games with him, saying no but signaling yes, putting up token resistance but always giving in.

Dinah had nothing but contempt for women who did that, and still it had come so easy to her that she hadn't even realized she was doing it. What was there about this young Adonis that drew her so strongly?

Todd leaned back in his seat and closed his eyes. She had a point. Why was he coming on to her so strong? It wasn't necessary in order to do the job he'd come here to do. She was a sweet, friendly, outgoing person, and it would have been easy for a trained investigator like himself to get information from her if he'd kept their relationship on the "brash-young-kid-big-sisterly-inclined-employer" basis that he'd intended.

Instead he'd messed everything up by letting his emotions get in the way. Each morning he woke with every intention of curbing his libido and getting on a casual footing with her, and every time he saw her, he forgot everything but how much he wanted her, how badly he needed her.

It was the needing that scared the hell out of him. He'd wanted women before, lots of times, but he'd never needed one the way he needed Dinah. It wasn't just his strong male urges he wanted to satisfy, either. He'd meant it both times he'd offered separate accommodations if she'd spend the weekend with him.

He wanted her with him even more than he wanted her in his bed.

His fingers were still wrapped tightly around her wrist, and he longed to raise her hand to his lips and kiss the soft warm palm. Instead, he steeled himself to release her and sat up.

"You're right," he said briskly. "I've been a nuisance. We'd better get moving. How about going on to Flagstaff when we get to the north end of the canyon and having dinner there?"

Flagstaff was a small city located at the junction of Interstates 17 and 40. As the hub of northern Arizona, many of the state's most popular tourist attractions—the Painted Desert, Petrified Forest and Grand Canyon—could be reached in one to two hours.

Todd and Dinah found a quaint restaurant tucked away in a grove of trees just outside of town. It had round maple tables covered with red-and-white checked cloths and a huge rock fireplace complete with a fire. Although the temperature had hovered around one hundred degrees in Phoenix, it had gotten progressively cooler as they drove through the mountains, and at seven thousand feet, Flagstaff was chilly in the evenings and the fire was welcome.

Todd and Dinah's dinner of country fried chicken was served family-style in thick bowls and platters, and when they'd finished eating, Todd pushed his plate away and sighed. "That's the closest I've come to a home-cooked meal since I left home." He grinned. "I think I'd better take a look and see if they've got my mother in the kitchen."

Dinah chuckled. "I take it she's a good cook?"

"The best. Her biscuits are a little bit lighter, and she serves a cheese sauce over her broccoli, but other than that this place is right up to her standards."

"Does your mother work?" Dinah asked, hungry to learn more about his background.

He shook his head. "No, at least not for a salary, but she spends a lot of time running the P.T.A., the Women's League at church, the hospital auxiliary, the—"

"I get the point," Dinah said with a laugh. "Has your family always lived in Florida?"

"Florida?" Todd said, before he remembered that he'd told her he'd come from that state. Actually, he'd been born and raised in Pasadena, California, but he didn't want her to connect him with the Los Angeles area where her husband had been tried and was now serving a prison term.

"Uh . . . yeah, Palm Beach," he amended quickly, hoping she hadn't caught his slip. "How about you? What do your parents do?"

He already knew, but again it was a good way to get her to talk about her past.

She took a sip of her coffee. "Mom and Dad are teachers. They're older than yours. Both are in their early sixties, so now that my little brother is out of college and on his own, I wouldn't be surprised if they decide to retire soon and travel."

Todd frowned. "You said your brother is twenty-two. I don't imagine he'd appreciate being called your 'little brother.'"

She looked at him warily, and he could have kicked himself. He was supposed to be probing her past, not starting another argument about age differences.

Thank heaven she chose not to challenge him. Instead she agreed. "You're right. He wouldn't. It's just that I find it hard to forget that I used to change his diapers."

Oh, great! Todd hoped to hell she wasn't thinking of *him* in diapers. It was time to change the subject.

He glanced at his watch. "Much as I hate to break this up, I think we'd better get started back toward Phoenix."

He reached over to where the waitress had put the check, but it wasn't there. His gaze searched the tabletop. "I thought the waitress brought the tab," he muttered.

"She did," Dinah said, and held it up for him to see. "I'm paying this time. You got lunch."

"I won't hear of it," he said. "I invited you to spend the day with me, and I'll pay for it. Besides, you fixed breakfast. Now give me the bill."

She crumpled it in her hand. "Don't be difficult, Todd," she said firmly. "It's not fair for you to have to bear all the expenses for this outing. You paid for the gas and the lunch, the least I can do is treat you to dinner."

He felt his temper rising and made an effort to curb it. "I'm not the one who's being difficult," he said. "You're my guest—"

"Look, what's the big deal?" She sounded perplexed. "Surely it hasn't escaped you that nowadays women often pay their share on dates. You're not going to make me believe that you went all through college without ever sharing the expense of going out with a girl."

He had to admit that she was right. His dates in college had nearly always picked up half the tab, and he'd thought nothing of it. Even now women often called him to say they had tickets to a rock concert or a play and would he go with them? He'd never been upset about that, so why was he so ticked off now?

He realized that Dinah was still talking. "I'm not going to let you spend your hard-earned money on me. You need all you can save for school expenses this fall. Either let me pay my own way or I won't go out with you anymore."

Damn but she had him rattled. He'd totally forgotten that he was supposed to be a destitute law student working his way through school.

He managed what he hoped was an embarrassed smile. "Well, if you're sure, but that means we get to go out twice as often."

"Todd Campbell, you're incorrigible," she said happily, and it finally occurred to him why he didn't want her to pay her way.

He wanted to take care of her. He wanted her to need him, too.

It was late when they got home, and Todd insisted on unlocking Dinah's door, going in to turn on the lights and making sure everything was all right.

"I'm used to being alone, Todd," she protested. "I don't need to be protected."

"Who says?" he growled as he flicked the light switch in every room. "All women, and men, too, for that matter, should be aware of the danger of attack and on guard against it. There are a lot of crazies out there, and don't you forget it."

"Yes, Daddy," she said with a giggle.

"Make fun of me all you want," he said, "but pay attention to what I'm telling you."

His concern for her was touching. "I always pay attention to you," she said huskily.

"Do you?" His voice dropped to a raspy murmur as he slipped one arm around her waist and raised his other hand to cup her cheek.

"Yes." It was little more than a whisper as she put her hands on his chest and felt the muscles under them contract. "Todd, I owe you an apology."

His thumb rubbed gently over her lips, setting up a slight friction that she felt all the way to her stomach. "What do you owe me an apology for?"

His tone was as unsteady as hers.

"Earlier today, in Oak Creek Canyon, I scolded you for being persistent and not leaving me alone." Her hands were moving in slow half circles on either side of his chest, and she felt his heart accelerate.

"You were right." His mouth brushed her forehead. "I should have respected your wishes. I'm sorry."

"No, I'm the one who's sorry." She ran her palms up to his shoulders. "I like it when you pester me. Can you forgive me for saying such hurtful things?"

He put his other arm around her and pulled her closer. "That depends," he said softly. "Are you sorry enough to give me a good-night kiss?"

She ran her tongue between her lips. "I might be." Her voice was low and throbbing. "Do you want an 'I'm sorry' kiss, or a 'thank you for the lovely day' kiss, or an 'I care about you' kiss?"

"All of the above," he murmured, and rubbed his cheek in her hair. "We can start with 'I'm sorry.'"

Slowly she raised her hands to position them on either side of his lowered head, then stroked her fingers through his silky blond curls as she stood on her toes and planted featherlike kisses first on one side of his mouth, then the other. His skin was smooth beneath her lips and smelled of fresh air and sunshine.

"I'm sorry that I was cross and unthinking," she whispered against his ear.

She let her hands trail down his face as her fingers gently sought out his forehead, his eyes, his nose and his chin before coming to rest at the sides of his neck. The hint of stubble was just rough enough to make her skin tingle.

"Now on to 'thank you.'" He was whispering, too, but their faces were so close that there was no need to speak louder.

Her questing fingers massaged the back of his neck while her thumbs rubbed the sensitive hollows under his ears. He'd been right with his comment earlier. It was infinitely more satisfactory caressing his warm flesh than it would have been exploring a statue.

Again she rose on her toes and kissed one side of his mouth, but this time she ran her lips slowly across his to get to the other side. When she'd finished, she tilted her head back a fraction of an inch, then kissed him full on the mouth.

He didn't move or respond, but a low moan escaped from deep in his throat, and his heart pounded against her breast.

Reluctantly she lowered herself back on her heels again, but now her palms moved over his shoulders, down his forearms and around to his back. He was all muscle. She could feel them flex as she rubbed her hands over them, and she resented the intrusion of his shirt between her flesh and his.

"Thank you for the lovely day." Her voice shook, and her words were a little garbled.

For a moment he just stood there moving slightly with the rhythm of her caress. Then he took a breath, as though trying to pull herself together, but when he spoke, his tone was raspy.

"I . . . I'm almost afraid to ask for this, but now can I have the 'I care about you' one?"

She was almost afraid to comply, but nothing short of dragging her away could have stopped her as she once more raised up on her toes. Putting her arms around his neck she pushed his head down a little more so she could touch each closed eyelid with her lips, then the tip of his nose. He shivered when she ignored his mouth and licked his chin, then nibbled at the pulse under his jaw.

His arms tightened around her, warning her that he'd about reached the limit of his endurance. She wasn't teasing him; she just wanted this to be as exciting for him as it was for her.

She raised her face to his and slowly ran the tip of her tongue over his lips—first top, then bottom—then opened her mouth slightly and covered his. By this time they were both trembling, and with an impatient groan he took over.

It was the sweetest, most arousing kiss she'd ever experienced. She could feel the leashed desire in him straining to get free, but he kept it under exquisite control as he tasted her and let her taste him.

His hands roamed lovingly over her back, down over the rise of her hips and up to the sides of her breasts. He made no suggestive moves and didn't try to touch her intimately, or blatantly make her aware of his aroused state, although there was no way he could hide it.

She relaxed in his arms and responded by caressing him in the same way. She'd never been kissed with such loving tenderness, and it was a thousand times more romantic than the greedy insistence she'd come to expect from men after they'd spent time and money on her.

It would be wonderful if she could just stay in Todd's arms like this forever.

But of course she couldn't, and it was Todd who eventually raised his head, although he cradled her face against his shoulder. He stroked his fingers through her long, thick fall of hair as she brushed her lips back and forth against the side of his neck.

For several minutes they just stood there holding each other without speaking until he finally sighed. "I'm overwhelmed," he said softly.

"So am I," she admitted, still breathless. "Oh, Todd, so am I. I never dreamed it would be like that."

"Me, neither." He sounded as bemused as she felt.

For a moment longer, they stood quietly, but then he straightened and stepped back, loosening their embrace. "It's time for me to leave, sweetheart," he said in a tone mixed with reluctance and determination. "Thank you for spending the day with me."

He released her, then put his hand under her chin and tilted her face upward. "Good night, Dinah," he said, and quickly touched his lips to hers. "Sleep well."

He turned and left without giving her a chance to answer.

Chapter Five

Todd was sweating as he hurried across the driveway. Not gentlemanly perspiration but honest-to-God sweat—the kind that left his palms wet and his shirt damp enough to make the air feel cool.

No woman had done that to him since he'd been an untried teenager. It had been sweet agony to just stand there while Dinah stroked and nibbled and kissed him, and not give in to his natural inclination to crush her in his arms and respond with all the wild exuberance she was kindling in him.

But it was worth it! Her gently questing touch that made his nerve ends quiver, the dampness of her tongue as she slowly taunted his mouth, and her soft, ripe lips under his that gave him what he craved and took what he longed to give, all combined to send him orbiting into euphoria. He wanted to click his heels in the air and sing at the top of his lungs about love and marriage and happy-ever-after.

His hand shook as he fitted the key in the lock of the front door of the recreation building.

Whoa there. Slow down, Campbell.

Love? Boy, he really had hit the sonic boom of reality and beyond. This had nothing to do with love. Like, certainly. He'd admit to being in *like* with Dinah Swensen. Lust? You bet. But love? No way. He couldn't possibly be in love with her; that would be a disaster of humongous proportions and didn't even bear thinking about.

And marriage? Sure, sometime. He eventually wanted to settle down with a wife and family, but he had a lot of years ahead of him before he'd be ready to give up his freewheeling ways and make that kind of commitment.

When he did, it wouldn't be with a woman who may have helped her first husband steal a fortune in gemstones.

That thought drained all the buoyancy out of him and left him unutterably depressed.

Todd got up early the next morning and dressed in dark dress slacks with a white shirt and maroon tie. He made a pot of coffee, then stationed himself in front of the window with it and a package of day-old doughnuts, to watch Dinah's apartment.

She hadn't told him where she was going today, so he'd have to find out for himself. The very idea disgusted him, but the time was drawing near when her ex-husband might be getting out of prison, and if she had the gems or knew where they were, she may be making contact with him.

If so, it was Todd's business to know about it.

Shortly after ten o'clock she came out looking like a fashion model in a navy linen suit with matching pumps and a crisp white blouse that had a lace collar and cuffs. He'd never seen her so dressed up this early in the day before, and was glad he'd also worn his Sunday best, just in case.

Feeling like a Peeping Tom, he watched her through the binoculars as she walked the block to the tenants' parking lot. Quickly he grabbed his sports jacket and cut through the building, out the back way across the pool area and down a different driveway. He reached the lot just as she was pulling out in her red Toyota and managed to catch up with her a few blocks from the complex.

He hadn't been exaggerating when he'd told her that his car was in good condition. It looked like the kind of old heap a graduate student might drive, but he'd taken it to a garage and had had it completely refitted with new, high-powered parts. It started with a touch, ran like a race car, and stopped on command.

He followed a couple of cars behind her as she drove to the Scottsdale area and parked in the lot beside a Spanish mission-style church. He pulled over to the curb a block away and parked under a shady tree.

He waited fifteen minutes, and when she didn't come around to the front and enter the church through the narthex, he got out of his car, put on his jacket and sauntered casually toward the building. People were streaming in now, and he joined them as they shook hands with the greeters just inside the doors, accepted an order of worship and entered the sanctuary.

Todd avoided the middle entrance in favor of the one that opened to the aisle on the far right, which was less conspicuous, and sat in one of the pews toward the back. It wasn't a large church, but it was filling up quickly, and he couldn't find Dinah in the sea of heads and shoulders. He hadn't seen her come in, but he knew that churches always had several entrances. She could have entered at the side or back.

The blue-robed choir marched into the loft behind the pulpit and the service was ready to begin. Todd's gaze continued to roam over the worshipers, and he was wondering if the church had been her destination after all, when he saw her. She entered through a side door at the front of the church with two men and a woman who was holding an infant wearing a long white dress that hung halfway to the floor.

They sat down together in the front pew, and the choir stood to sing their opening anthem. Todd breathed a sigh of relief and glanced at the order of worship in his hand. As he'd suspected, there was a baptism scheduled just before the pastoral prayer.

Dinah must be the godmother, which meant she was closely associated with these people. Were they relatives or just close friends? She hadn't said anything about having relatives here.

When the time arrived, the minister announced that Wayne and Vickie Wagner were presenting their baby son for baptism, and that Dinah Swensen and Carter Longstreet were the godparents. Todd filed the names away in his quick memory along with a reminder to find out who they were and how they figured in Dinah's life.

Later, when the congregation stood to sing the last hymn, he left as unobtrusively as possible and hurried to the parking lot. A hasty examination of the area assured him that the only entrance and exit were the front ones, and he returned to his car to wait until Dinah left.

It took a while, and most of the cars had been driven away before her red Toyota came out of the lot and turned down the street away from him. He followed her through upper-middle-class Scottsdale to an expensive-looking, white rambling ranch-style home, where she parked behind several other cars at the curb and went in.

Todd drove on past, then made a U-turn at the end of the block to park behind another car. He was far enough away that he probably wouldn't be noticed, and still he could see everyone who came and went.

For an hour he sat there watching people come, but no one left. Hunger pangs reminded him that it was past lunchtime, and that that was probably what was going on in the house—Sunday brunch. A party in celebration of the baby's christening.

He got out of the car and strolled across the street and toward the house. When he reached it, he could hear music and voices coming from the backyard as well as the exuberant sounds of people diving and splashing in a swimming pool.

Damn, this was going to go on all afternoon.

He walked on past the house, then turned at the end of the block and walked around it to get back to his car. This was an affluent neighborhood, and the residents wouldn't take kindly to a stranger loitering around. A glance at his watch told him it was two-thirty. He might as well go back to his room and wait for Dinah to come home.

During the long afternoon, with the aid of the telephone book and some well-placed inquiries, he found out that Wayne Wagner and Carter Longstreet were lawyers who were partners in one of Phoenix's upscale law firms. Wagner was the attorney who handled legal matters for the developers who owned the properties Dinah managed.

The real shocker was Wagner's wife, Victoria. *She was a free-lance jewelry designer!*

It could just be coincidence—probably was—but that discovery shook Todd to his very soul. Little by little his confidence in Dinah was being chipped away. First, she hadn't told him the true story of her divorce, then, the guy who had been a close friend of hers and probably of her ex-husband's had appeared. And now, she'd just become the godmother to the child of a woman who knew as much as Anson Erhardt did about precious gems.

Coincidence? Possibly, but how many fortuitous incidents can happen before they stop being coincidences and start being suspicious?

At six, he began to get uneasy. How long could it take to eat lunch and go for a swim?

By eight, he was walking the floor. What if there'd been an accident? Dinah had admitted that she wasn't a good swimmer.

At nine, he got in his car and headed back to Scottsdale. If she was still there, he'd better find out what was going on. He'd wait and follow her home to make sure she got there okay.

All the cars were gone from in front of the Wagner home, including Dinah's, and everything was quiet.

Todd swore and hit the steering wheel with his fist. Where in hell was she?

It was ten forty-five before Todd got back to the apartment complex, and Dinah's car still wasn't in the lot. Apprehension coiled like a knot in his stomach, and he didn't know whether to be scared or mad . . . not that he had a choice. He was both!

He parked his car and decided to sit in it and wait for her. The lot was dimly lit so he wouldn't have to worry about being seen.

God, but he hoped she was all right.

By eleven-fifteen, he was pacing up and down the parking lot when he saw her Toyota coming. The bright red glowed under the lights, and he'd have known it anywhere. His relief was so great that he forgot to move, and he managed to duck out of sight between two cars only seconds before her headlights swept the spot where he'd been standing as she turned in.

While she was parking, another car, a white Cadillac, turned in behind her and stopped.

What was going on? Was the joker in that Caddy harassing her?

As he watched, tensed to spring in case of trouble, Dinah got out of her car, walked over to the other one and got in.

Now where was she going? Now that he'd gotten a good look, he recognized the driver as Carter Longstreet, the lawyer who had stood as godfather of the baby. Surely this wasn't the old scenario of following the lady home so she could leave her car, then taking her back to his place to spend the night?

Todd had done that a number of times, but Dinah had sounded so sincere when she'd told him she'd been celibate since her divorce.

The Cadillac backed out of the lot and headed slowly up the street toward Dinah's apartment. Todd let out the breath he'd been holding. Of course, he was just driving her on home.

He followed the car on foot and, sure enough, it stopped in front of Dinah's place and they both got out. Todd was on the other side of the street, next to the recreation building, and he scrunched up close to it where his outline couldn't be seen.

Dinah's porch light was on, and Todd saw her hand Longstreet her key. He unlocked her door and stepped inside to turn on her living room light, then came back out and took her in his arms.

Todd tensed as Dinah put her arms around the other man's neck and lifted her face for his kiss. It was like a kick in the gut as Todd watched the embrace, and it was all he could do not to rush across the driveway and tear them apart.

When they broke off the kiss, Longstreet continued to hold her, and in the stillness of the desert night Todd could hear the faint murmur of voices but couldn't make out what was being said. If that guy talked his way in, Todd wasn't sure he had enough control not to go over and toss him out bodily.

Fortunately he wasn't tested. Longstreet left after a few minutes, and the couple called good-night to each other as he headed for his car and Dinah went in the apartment.

Todd heaved a sigh of relief and went to his room, but he couldn't erase the picture in his mind of Dinah kissing another man, and he didn't sleep worth a damn.

Monday turned out to be one of those days when Dinah wished she'd never gotten into property management. It seemed that everything that could go wrong with apartments did. Plumbing, air conditioning, and the coup de grace was a fire that gutted one of the units in the singles' complex in Tempe.

She'd been notified of that shortly before lunch and had spent the rest of the afternoon over there with the fire, police and insurance investigators. By the time she got back to her own place there were half a dozen calls on her answering machine that had to be returned and dealt with. At eight o'clock, when she finished with those, she realized that she hadn't eaten since breakfast and was hungry and exhausted.

She was sprawled on the couch, trying to work up enough energy to fix herself something to eat when the telephone rang. She was tempted not to answer it, but her conscience got the better of her. After all, that's what she was paid for.

She picked up the receiver, and it was Todd. Just the sound of his voice made her shiver with pleasure.

"I heard about the fire in your Tempe complex," he said. "Been trying to call you ever since you got home, but your line's been busy. Have you had dinner?"

"No, I haven't," she answered. "I was just sitting here wishing a genie would bring it to me."

"Your wish is my command. What do you like? Hamburgers? Pizza? Something from the deli? Or would you rather go out?"

A warm wave of gratitude and affection engulfed her. "Oh, Todd, I wasn't hinting—"

"No, but I'm inviting. There's a little place—"

"I'm too tired to go out," she interrupted, "but I'd love to eat with you, if you don't mind bringing something in. Anything will do. I'm easy to please."

"Great," he said. "Just give me half an hour or so."

While he was gone, Dinah changed out of her slim skirt, prim blouse and panty hose into powder blue shorts and a matching tank top. She briefly considered slipping her feet into her white sandals, but discarded the idea in favor of going barefoot.

Todd arrived in twenty minutes with steaming hot chicken, mashed potatoes and gravy, coleslaw, biscuits and two individual coconut cream pies.

"Bless both you and the Colonel," she said happily as she took the containers out of the white sacks and put them on the table, which she'd already set with dishes and silverware. "It smells delicious."

It was delicious. Dinah had developed a taste for takeout foods since she'd been living alone. Between that and microwaved frozen dinners, she seldom cooked anymore. It depressed her to go to all the trouble of fixing a dinner for just one person.

Todd had bought a whole bucket of chicken, and while they ate, they talked. "I saw you leave yesterday morning," he said. "You looked so pretty in that blue suit."

Dinah smiled, grateful for the compliment. "Thank you. I went to church. Friends of mine had their baby baptized, and they asked me to be the godmother."

"Lucky baby," he murmured. "You must be very close to the parents."

"Yes," she admitted. "They're the best friends I have in Phoenix. Wayne is the attorney who handles legal matters for the properties I manage. He introduced me to his wife, Vickie, and we've been friends ever since."

"Is his wife an attorney, too?"

She shook her head. "No, she designs jewelry, but right now she hasn't much time for anything but the baby. He's only two months old."

"No, I don't suppose she does," Todd agreed. "What did you do after church?"

"Oh, Wayne and Vickie had a group of relatives and friends over to their home for a pool party, and later I went to a movie."

He frowned. "You shouldn't go to movies alone at night. It's not safe."

"Oh, I wasn't alone," she assured him. "I went with a friend."

Todd's eyebrows raised. "A date?"

She swallowed and hesitated before she answered. It occurred to her that he was coming awfully close to prying.

"I guess you could call it that," she said, "but now suppose you tell me what you did yesterday."

For just a moment he looked startled, but then he grinned. "Oh, not much. I slept most of the morning." His voice lowered and softened. "After that good-night kiss you gave me, I tossed and turned till I finally fell asleep about dawn."

Dinah felt the warm flush that she knew must glow pink on her cheeks, and she ducked her head as she quickly changed the subject.

When they'd finished eating, Todd announced that he had two new videotapes that he hadn't watched yet. "One of them is the latest Academy Award winner, and the other is the classic Laurence Olivier/Merle Oberon version of *Wuthering Heights.*"

"*Wuthering Heights!*" Dinah almost clapped her hands with glee. "I love and adore *Wuthering Heights,* but I haven't seen it in ages."

"I thought you might," he said smugly. "That's why I got it. I hoped maybe I could entice you to watch it with me."

"I'm enticed, I'm enticed," she assured him happily. "You go get it while I clean up the kitchen."

A short time later, they settled down together on the sofa as the opening credits of the black-and-white movie flashed on the television screen. Dinah was aware that her body and Todd's were touching as she leaned back, but she couldn't force herself to move away. Instead she basked in the warmth that radiated from him.

Long ago she'd stopped kidding herself that her interest in him was sisterly, but just because her long-neglected hormones were beginning to rebel didn't mean that she had to be carried away by their insistent prodding.

"I first read this book in junior high," she said with a sigh. "It was an English assignment, and since then I must have read it at least half a dozen times as well as watch the movie every chance I get."

Todd turned slightly and put his arm around her, then kissed her on the nose. "You, my sweet Dinah, are an incurable romantic," he said tenderly.

"I know," she admitted. "I can't help it. Forbidden love is so sad."

His arm tightened around her, and he settled her comfortably against him. "Yes, it is." His tone was suddenly solemn. "I suspect it's a lot more tantalizing and exciting in fiction than in real life. Don't forget that Heathcliff and Cathy were never happy or fulfilled in their love."

Dinah felt a cool touch of apprehension, like a faint breeze at the back of her neck, and she instinctively snuggled closer to Todd as they watched the story of the star-crossed lovers unfold.

She quickly became engrossed in the movie, but still she was tinglingly aware of his arms holding her, the firm muscles of his chest beneath her back and his wandering hand that had slowly worked its way up from her waist to support the underside of her unencumbered breast.

She knew she should stop him. She also knew that she should have worn a bra beneath her skimpy tank top, and suspected that subconsciously she'd wanted to tantalize him when she'd dressed this way. Besides, he made her feel so good, and he wasn't being offensive at all.

She turned in his arms, and her hand settled on his chest. As usual he was wearing a T-shirt and cutoffs, and the thin cotton between her palm and his bare skin was more of an irritant than a barrier.

Todd had a magnificent body. There wasn't an ounce of flab anywhere, and muscles rippled whenever he moved. He wasn't hairy, only a light covering on his chest and legs, and that was so blond as to be almost unnoticeable unless you happened to be running your fingers through it.

Good heavens, where had that thought come from?

As though reading her mind, Todd pulled his shirt out of his jeans and repositioned her hand under it. It occurred to her to resist, but that was as far as it got. As soon as her hand settled in the soft hair on the warm flesh, she knew she wasn't going to pull it away.

Instead she let her fingers wander slowly over the breadth of his ribs before circling first one hard nipple, then the other. His breathing speeded up as did his heartbeat, and carefully so as not to dislodge her, he drew her tank top loose and slid his hand underneath and up to cup her bare breast.

His palm was wide and firm and just rough enough to add an extra dimension to the sensual pleasure that rippled through her. With a little gasp she clutched at his chest hair and felt him wince.

"I'm sorry," she said, and quickly pulled her hand away.

"Don't be," he murmured thickly, and caressed the sensitive hollow at the side of her throat with his lips. "I want your touch."

He straightened up and released her, then tugged his shirt over his head and tossed it aside. "That's better," he said as he gathered her into his arms again, and laid her hand on his bare belly just above his waistband.

Oh, my! The jolt she received went all through her. This time she really should protest. Those shorts he was wearing were cut pretty low, and the muscles in his stomach clenched and unclenched beneath her questing palm.

Not that his were the only ones. Hers had tightened in all her most intimate places, and she found it difficult to sit still. Yes, this time she'd definitely have to call a halt. Any minute now she'd remove her hand and insist that he stop stroking her throbbing breast and rolling her hardened nipples between his gentle fingers....

The sound-track music reached a thundering crescendo and captured Dinah's attention as Heathcliff, in a towering rage, mounted his horse and galloped across the barren moors and away from the child/woman and her wastrel brother whose torment he could no longer endure.

It apparently distracted Todd, too, because he stopped actively arousing her. Although he continued to hold her breast, and she left her hand resting on his abdomen, they made an effort to relax and watch the movie.

When, at last, the spirits of Cathy and Heathcliff, freed from their earthly restraints, walked happily across the moors toward an eternity with each other, Todd picked up the remote control and switched it off. Dinah sighed. "That's such a beautiful ending. I always get goose bumps when I watch it."

"Well, yes and no," he said as he settled back with her still in his arms. "It may be a romantic conclusion for a movie, but there aren't many real men and women who want to wait until they're spirits to consummate their love. I'd have liked the story better if Heathcliff and Catherine had just said to hell with what other people wanted or thought and had gone off together while they were still young and alive."

Todd's hand settled on Dinah's bare thigh and thrilled a whole new set of nerve endings. He nibbled at her earlobe, and when he spoke again, his voice was husky with yearning. "I'm not the most patient man in the world, and I've been waiting forty-eight hours for another of your special brand of kisses."

Slowly he caressed her face with his lips until, by the time he settled on her mouth, she was breathless with anticipation. For a self-confessed impatient man, his control was marvelous. He brushed her lips with his, and hers opened of their own accord to welcome his questing tongue. It sought out her dark, moist recesses, and he tasted musky and male.

Her tongue welcomed his and stroked it until, with a low groan, his began the little thrusting motions that made her arch against him and dig her fingers into his shoulders. His hand moved up and down her leg, and she bent her knee and brought it up to position it against his abdomen. His hard maleness pressed into her shin, and he shuddered and clutched at her thigh.

"Oh, God, Dinah," he moaned. "Have you any idea what you do to me? You're so soft and cuddly and responsive, and I think I just may die of pure, undiluted pleasure."

She started to remove her leg. "I . . . I didn't mean . . ." she stammered before he clutched her calf and guided it back where it had been.

"No, don't," he pleaded. "Leave it just like that. I'm not going to do anything you don't want me to."

He cradled her against him and trailed kisses down her throat until he was stopped by the low-cut, U-shaped neckline of her tank top at the rise of her breasts. Dinah's hands were on the sides of his head, guiding him, and she twisted, pulling the loose-fitting bodice down and to the side so that one breast was exposed to his eager lips.

He teased her nipple, licking and nipping lightly and sending tiny pinpoints of flame up and down her spine. She stroked his head and squirmed beneath the onslaught of exultation until he finally took her fully into his mouth and sucked gently.

She relaxed, and her breath came in purring gasps as she continued to caress his head, neck, shoulders and back. He rocked them gently back and forth, and his suckling tugged at muscles deep in her core.

She wanted him. Wanted him not only in her bed, but in her heart and in her soul. She wanted him badly enough to give herself to him right here and now, with no promises or commitments or assurances of happy-ever-after.

He needed her physically now, and in a few minutes when he could no longer control that need, she wouldn't try to stop him. She'd give herself to him completely and unconditionally because she was past the point of rational thought.

Todd fought to hang on to his sanity as his body screamed for fulfillment. He had to stop now, but he wasn't sure he could. Dinah was driving him over the brink with her strong little hands that alternately soothed and aroused him until he was wild with need. She was soft and pliable in his arms, and the mewling noises she made deep in her throat assured him that her need was almost as great as his.

A combination like that was lethal, and Todd wasn't used to having to deny his strong urges. He'd never before come this far when he knew he wasn't going to complete it, and he was in agony.

It took every ounce of his willpower, but he managed to remove his mouth from her full, sweet-tasting breast and disengage her arms from around his neck so he could straighten up. She clung to him and nuzzled the side of his throat, eliciting a cry of actual pain as he struggled not to give in and take her right there on the couch.

The cry must have penetrated her fog, because she blinked and slowly opened her passion-filled eyes. "Wh-what's the matter?" Her voice was heavy with the same desire that was tormenting him, and again he strained to fight back the overwhelming craving to make love to her tonight and worry about it tomorrow.

"Honey, if we don't stop now, we won't be able to." His tone was raw with frustration.

Again she blinked, and this time her eyes were clearer. "But I wasn't protesting," she said plaintively, and nearly broke his heart. He had to make sure she didn't think he didn't want her.

"I know, darling, but I promised I wouldn't seduce you, and that's exactly what I was doing." His breathing was ragged. "I wanted you so much that I came on too strong and didn't give you a chance to object."

He moved farther away and ran his fingers through his hair in a gesture of self-disgust. "You're a passionate woman, Dinah, and if and when you come to me, I want it to be of your own free will, not because I'm taking advantage of that passion."

She looked as if he'd slapped her, and he silently cursed his awkwardness. Where was that celebrated charm when he so desperately needed it?

His arms ached to pull her back into them, and he stood up before he could do just that. "Dinah, you're an experienced woman. You know how much I wanted you."

He sounded gruff, and that hadn't been his intent.

"Yes," she said, expressionlessly.

"Then you understand?"

"Yes." She was speaking in a monotone, and she still hadn't moved.

Todd knew he'd better get out of there quick before all his good intentions melted in the hell of his own making.

"I'm going to leave now," he said. "Not because I want to, but because there are things you should know before..."

From inside his head a voice sounded loud and clear. *Shut up, Campbell, and get out of here before you blow the whole damn case!*

He clamped his mouth shut, then turned and left before the temptation to do just that became too great to resist.

Dinah slumped against the soft cushions and closed her eyes as wave after wave of humiliation washed over her.

How could she have behaved like the stereotypical sex-starved divorcée who can't wait to get a man in her bed? No wonder she'd scared Todd off! He'd probably just wanted a little making out, and she'd practically ravished him.

She turned her face into the cushion and shuddered. It had taken a while, but she'd finally learned her lesson. From this moment on, Todd Campbell was an employee and nothing else. She'd be friendly with him because that's the way she treated all the people she worked with, but no more dates, no more touching and especially no more kissing.

In a few days she'd tell him that she needed the storage room back and ask him to find an apartment somewhere else as soon as possible.

She'd be damned if she'd wind up one of those frustrated, lonely females who came on to younger men in a frenzied effort to recapture their fading youth.

Chapter Six

When Todd returned to his room during lunch break the
following day, there was a message on the telephone answering machine from the fax service he used telling him
that material had come through for him and was being
held for pickup.

He yawned and rubbed his burning eyes. He'd lost more
sleep over Dinah Swensen in the two weeks he'd known her
than he'd lost over any other woman in his entire life.

After he'd left her last night, he'd walked for hours, then
done ten laps in the Olympic-size pool, but even so, he'd
lain awake until almost morning, unable to erase the feel
and the taste and the scent of her from his mind. This situation was getting out of control.

If Wesley Nelson ever found out that Todd was this
emotionally involved with the suspect he was investigating, Todd would be taken off the case, and rightly so. If he
had any sense at all, he'd ask to be replaced, but he
couldn't do it.

Not only was the thought of never seeing her again too painful to contemplate, but the idea of some other operative spying on her was intolerable.

It was almost as if Dinah Swensen Erhardt was fated to be *the woman* in his life, and he had no choice in the matter. They were playing out a modern-day Greek tragedy where the course for disaster was set and there was no changing it. If she was innocent of any wrongdoing in the gem theft, she'd never forgive him for his deception, and if she was guilty, she'd hate him for sending her to prison.

And he'd hate himself even more.

He dressed and made a hurried trip to the fax service. As he'd expected, the material was the report he'd requested on Bernard Rose. Back in his room he read it over while eating the hamburger he'd picked up on his way home.

The information confirmed what Dinah had already told him. Bernard Rose had first surfaced in Los Angeles in 1976 when he went to work as general manager for an automobile dealership. Four years later the owner sold the business to Bernie and retired. Everything was in order. He'd borrowed a large sum of money, but it was all aboveboard and he'd long since paid it back with interest.

A routine police check of him at the time of Erhardt's trial revealed that he'd had a wife, Sarah, and they'd been close friends of Dinah and Anson. They'd even testified as character witnesses on Anson's behalf, but there was nothing to link them with the jewel theft.

A dealer who sold cars had little in common, business-wise, with a gemologist who cut and mounted precious stones. Apparently he was what Dinah had said he was—a close friend who'd stopped by to see her on his way through Phoenix.

Todd didn't see Dinah again until Wednesday evening. She hadn't come down to the pool area as she sometimes did, and she'd been gone when he got off work on Tuesday. It was almost midnight before she'd come home, and by then it had been too late for him to casually saunter over and ask where she'd been. Instead, he'd gone to bed and had tried to calm his frayed nerves enough to sleep.

When he got off his shift on Wednesday, Dinah's car was in the lot, and Todd hurried to shower and dress so he could catch her before she could avoid him again, if that's what she was doing. All the while he prayed that he could remember to keep his mind on the investigation, and his hands off her.

After grabbing a couple of colas from the machine, he hurried across the street and rang her bell. She opened the door, and for just a second he thought he saw despair in her wide blue eyes, but then she smiled and it was gone.

Good. She'd accepted his explanation for not staying with her Monday night.

"Hello, Todd," she said, but made no move to unlock the screen. "Is there something I can do for you?"

He grinned. "Well, yes, now that you mention it, you can invite me in."

For a long moment she hesitated, then flicked the lock. "All right, but I'm really awfully busy."

"Not too busy for an ice-cold drink, surely." He held up the two cans.

She turned away and headed through the small dining room to the tiny kitchen. "I guess I can take a break long enough for that." Her tone was firmly businesslike as she took glasses from the cupboard and filled them with ice.

"I'm catching up on my bookwork," she explained, indicating the jumble of papers and ledgers on the table. "No matter how hard I try, I never manage to stay current."

She was babbling, but he played along to see where she was leading, if anywhere. "There's always something to take the fun out of life," he said flippantly as he accepted the glass of cola with ice and followed her into the living room.

"Yes," she said in the same dead tone she'd used Monday night. "I've noticed that."

This time he knew he hadn't mistaken the look of sadness on her lovely face as she sat down in the chair, leaving the sofa for him. Did she think she couldn't trust him to behave if she sat beside him?

Something was wrong, but she obviously wasn't going to tell him what unless he pried it out of her.

So, okay, he deserved her distrust. He never should have let things go as far as they had Monday. She had good reason for not believing that he could control himself.

"Honey, if you're upset about Monday night, I—"

She raised her head and looked at him. "Monday? Don't be silly, Todd, I'm not blaming you. Actually, I'm more embarrassed than anything. I don't usually act like a tart."

"Dinah!" Hearing her call herself by that crude term brought him to his feet. "How can you say such a thing?"

She looked startled and also stood. "Calm down," she said. "I suppose it is a little harsh, but you know what I mean. I guess I've missed the . . . the conjugal part of marriage more than I thought. I owe you a debt of gratitude for having the good sense to stop."

Good sense! Dear Lord, she still didn't understand what it had cost him to tear himself away from her. On the other hand what had she meant by that crack about the conjugal side . . ."

"Are you saying that all you wanted was sex, and any man would have filled the bill?" His voice was harsh.

A rosy flush suffused her face and made him feel like a heel until she took a deep breath and answered. "I wouldn't put it quite that bluntly."

Her tone had cooled considerably. "Don't sell yourself short. You're an extremely beguiling guy, and I've been without a man in my life for a long time. I'm afraid I got carried away with your practiced lovemaking. You're very good."

"Practiced!" Todd practically yelled the offending word. "You think I was just making a move on you to keep in practice!"

Through a haze of shock and pain he knew he was handling this badly. He should put a lid on his temper and take control of the situation, but, damn it, she didn't fight fair. How could she trivialize what they'd had together? It was so far beyond anything he'd experienced before....

"No, of course not," she answered calmly. "I suspect that I'm the one who seduced you. There was no doubt about my willingness...."

She rambled on, but he deliberately shut out what she was saying. He hated her cool, rational, postmortem of that extra special time they'd shared.

Was he wrong? Had he just imagined that she was as strongly attracted to him as he was to her? And what difference did it make anyway?

He wasn't here to build a relationship with Dinah Swensen; he was supposed to be investigating her, and time was running out. He didn't have the leisure to quarrel with her. He had to keep the lines of communication open on the chance that she wasn't as innocent as he hoped to God she was.

It must have been the silence that interrupted his brooding and brought him back to his senses. Dinah had quit talking and was apparently waiting for him to comment.

"Uh...look, honey," he began, at a loss as to how to respond when he hadn't heard most of what she'd said. "Why don't we just concede that we were both at fault and go on from there? Have dinner with me? I found this great Mexican place that has the best—"

"I'm sorry, Todd, but that's out of the question," she interrupted. "I told you, I have all this bookwork to do, and tomorrow afternoon I have to drive to Tucson for a three-day conference—"

"You're going out of town?" He felt as if she'd just knocked the breath out of him.

Her eyes widened. "Yes, to a property-management conference. I'll post the name and phone number of the firm I work for on the bulletin board in the rec room. Someone will be on call until I get back in case a problem arises or there's an emergency."

The private investigator side of him automatically snapped to alert. Was she telling the truth about where she was going and why? Or did this little trip have something to do with her ex-husband's upcoming parole hearing? He felt sick.

"I don't give a damn who's on call," he grated, his quick temper dampened by his insidious suspicion. "Why didn't you mention it earlier? Were you planning to leave without saying a word to me about it?"

She looked down and slightly past him. "I wasn't aware that I had to ask your permission, but I'm telling you now. I'll also leave the name and number of my temporary replacement on my telephone answering machine. If you need me, there will be someone available to respond."

A weary sigh escaped him as he turned away and headed for the door. "If I need you, Dinah, it won't do any good to call in a substitute. What I need from you, only you can give me.''

Dinah managed to hold up until Todd shut the door behind him, then she slumped into the nearest chair and put her face in her hands.

Had it really been necessary to be so cold and uncaring to him? He was such a sweet, friendly man, eager to experience all of life's pleasures, but also willing to expose himself to the disappointments that were often intertwined with the joy. Surely she could have been kinder, let him down more gently.

No, that didn't work. She'd tried it at other times, but he didn't discourage easily. Probably because he sensed that she didn't really want to discourage him.

Who was she kidding? He didn't have to sense it; she'd made her need for him plain Monday night, and he'd backed away.

For her own protection she had to put distance between them. That's why she'd volunteered to baby-sit her tiny godson last night so that Wayne and Vickie Wagner could attend a party.

She hadn't wanted to face Todd then, but knew she'd have to soon. That's when she'd planned her strategy, and also when she'd decided to go to the conference in Tucson after all. It was a last-minute change of plans, but it would keep her away for three days over the weekend when it would be most difficult to avoid Todd if she were home.

She still couldn't trust herself not to melt at his touch.

Todd didn't see Dinah before she left for Tucson on Thursday, but he hired another operative to follow her from the time she left Phoenix until she returned. He hated exposing her to another man's surveillance, but he couldn't get away. There were things he had to do while she was gone.

She didn't come down to the pool to say goodbye, and by the time his shift was over, she'd left.

Now he was faced with another odious task, that of searching her apartment. He'd put it off, hoping she'd tell him what he needed to know so he wouldn't have to, but time was running out, and he'd never have an opportunity like this again.

For the first time he seriously considered admitting to Wes that he was too emotionally involved with Dinah Swensen to be objective and ask to be taken off the case. He could pack his things, leave a note telling her his parents needed him, and catch a flight to L.A. tonight. It was the coward's way out, sneaking off with no notice while she was away, but maybe it would be best for both of them.

Possibly so, but he knew he wasn't going to do it. Things had gone too far, both personally and professionally, to turn back now. He could never abandon her completely to the dispassionate probing of an insensitive operative.

Just the thought made his blood run cold, but even more agonizing was the idea of losing her. To never again see approval in her sparkling blue eyes, or run his fingers through the shining silk of her golden hair, or feel her soft, tempting curves pressed against the urgent need of his throbbing body.

He was in an intolerable situation. His whole being revolted at the thought of walking away from her, but what would he do if he proved that she was an accomplice in the gem theft?

There was no way in hell he could help send her to prison!

Todd's alarm went off shortly before daybreak on Friday morning, but he was already awake. He got up and dressed in his scruffy jeans and T-shirt, extracted a miniature leather tool case and an equally small camera from beneath his clean underwear in the drawer, and let himself out of the building.

The sky was beginning to lighten as he crossed the empty, silent driveway and strode boldly up to Dinah's front door. He didn't want to be seen skulking around. Better to act as though he was calling on her and didn't know she wasn't home.

Opening the screen door, he made quick work of picking the lock on the other one with his tiny tools. Inside, he moved around the front rooms to get his bearings.

In the past, his trained eye had skimmed over the furniture, wall hangings, books, magazines and knickknacks, but he hadn't had the opportunity to really examine anything. He'd never been in the bedroom or the bathroom, and the only time he'd entered the office was the day he was hired.

Not a very thorough scrutiny for a private investigator. He'd been more interested in the woman than in her surroundings.

This time he went through the place like a vacuum cleaner, leaving no article untouched. As he searched, he noted that her furniture was inexpensive but well cared for, the pictures were mostly framed posters of famous paintings, her choice of novels was predominantly paperback mysteries and romances and according to her tapes and records, her favorite singers were Judy Collins and Julio Iglesias, with a few Crystal Gayle tapes for a change of pace.

He made a mental note to introduce her to soft rock.

As he was going through the papers in her office files, the phone rang. He jumped and dropped the folder he was holding. Damn! Would he ever get used to this business?

His nerves were always on edge when he was violating someone else's property.

The answering machine gave its little spiel, and the person on the other end hung up without leaving a message. Todd picked up the folder and continued his search but found nothing that was in any way suspicious.

Dinah was an exceptionally neat person, and he was careful to put everything he'd touched back where he found it. He didn't want her to know that her apartment had been searched.

In the bathroom he dismantled some of the plumbing with no results, and it wasn't until he was halfway through her bedroom that he received a sickening shock.

He'd left this room until last. It was where a woman would keep her most personal things, and he felt like the lowest form of life for violating Dinah's privacy.

Starting with the closet, he checked everything until he finally came to the dresser. It was the most distasteful to inspect. These drawers would contain her intimate clothing, and there was something indecent about a man pawing through a woman's silky underwear. Especially Dinah's. He'd beat to a pulp any other guy he caught doing it.

On top was a framed picture of Dinah with an older couple and a younger man. Obviously her family. They all had that same healthy Nordic beauty, and he had a gut feeling that Dinah's children would also inherit it.

He muttered an oath and forcefully shifted his thoughts to the drawer he was opening. It was shallow and contained cosmetics and toiletries. He probed the jars, bottles and tubes with one of his slender tools but found only the creams, liquids and powders that were supposed to be there.

In the drawer below it he found a small locked jewel box beneath a pile of silk panties. The lock was a joke and yielded easily to his handy pick.

Inside were a diamond ring and matching wedding band plus the jeweled combs she'd worn a couple of times when she'd been with him. According to the inventory he'd been given by the insurance company, all three items had been examined at the time Erhardt had been arrested and found not to be part of the unset diamonds that had been stolen, but they were valuable. Did the fact that she kept them at home mean she didn't have a safe-deposit box?

The last drawer was deep and contained bulky clothing, but underneath a fluffy sweater was a white gift box. Todd removed it, then put it on top of the dresser and opened it. There were several layers of tissue paper before his hand connected with a hard, round article, and he withdrew it.

He blinked and drew in his breath. The object in his palm wasn't round but egg-shaped. It appeared to be enamel, heavily encrusted with gold. Todd knew little about precious gems and metals, or art objects, but this had to be real gold. If so, it was worth a lot of money on today's market.

Two million dollars' worth?

Oh, dear God, no! Was it possible for Dinah to have sold the gems and invested the money in something like this that wouldn't be connected with them but could be resold when her husband got out of prison?

On the other hand if this was worth all that money, she surely wouldn't keep it in her dresser drawer, would she?

With a cold feeling of dread Todd carefully rewrapped the precious object and put it back in the box. He'd have to take it with him and have it appraised quickly so that he could put it back before she came home.

It was time for the pool gates to be opened and his swim class to start by the time he left the apartment and dashed across the street to change into his trunks, but it wasn't his tardiness that caused his heart to pound with anxiety.

Had Dinah been playing him for a fool all along? Was she just amusing herself with him to pass the time until her husband was released on parole? Had she been in on the heist all along and now expected to reap the rewards?

The property-management conference ended on Sunday with a brunch, and shortly afterward, Dinah and several of the acquaintances she'd made during the past three days were gathered to say goodbye in the lobby of the luxury hotel where the event had been held.

"Don't forget, Dinah, you're having dinner with me Tuesday night," reminded Jeff Marshall, a dark-haired man in his late thirties who managed office buildings in Apache Junction, a small city at the foot of the Superstitions, a group of mountains a few miles east of Phoenix. "I'll pick you up at seven."

"How could I forget?" she asked graciously, hiding her reluctance. "I'll be ready."

It wasn't that there was anything wrong with Jeff, she thought as she claimed her car and drove away. He was a nice guy, single, handsome and bright, but she had no desire to go out with any man except Todd.

Damn, she must be going through an early midlife crisis. Why had she let herself become attached to a kid who didn't even know for sure what he wanted? The only way she could think of to get over him was to date other, more mature men and hope the infatuation would pass.

Not that she'd had any luck so far. If she'd expected that putting distance between them would help, she'd been abysmally wrong. Every time she'd seen a young, blond man, her heart had leaped until she'd come to her senses and realized that it wasn't Todd.

It had been a miserable weekend. She couldn't erase from her mind that last image of him looking so hurt and dejected as he'd walked away from her. Now she couldn't control her excitement at the thought of seeing him again, or at least knowing that he was just across the driveway.

Such adolescent thoughts were unacceptable. She was going to have to get a grip on her emotions and start acting her age. He was still young enough to be excused for his boyish behavior, but she was old enough to know better.

At four o'clock that Sunday afternoon Todd was sitting by the window in his room, watching for Dinah to come home and listening to a Rod Stewart tape on his stereo. To his great relief, the operative he'd hired to follow her had reported that there was indeed a property-management conference in Tucson and she had attended every one of the sessions.

The appraisal of the gold-encrusted object he'd found in her bedroom hadn't been as satisfactory. He'd taken it to Orville Fischbeck, a well-known art appraiser, during his lunch hour on Friday and told the man that he was having the article appraised for insurance purposes and couldn't leave it there or let it out of his possession.

Unfortunately, since it wasn't something that could be immediately identified, the appraisal would take time. Fischbeck closed his offices on Saturday and Sunday so he'd examined it extensively at the time, then had taken photographs to help with his evaluation and had told Todd to come back late Monday afternoon.

It had been frustrating, but there had been nothing he could do but wait. Meanwhile the suspense hadn't dulled the ache of missing Dinah, and he was eagerly anticipating her return when there was a knock on his door.

He hurried to open it, knowing it couldn't be Dinah but hoping that it was.

It wasn't. It was Lynette something, the sexy blond seventeen-year-old who followed him around at the pool and couldn't keep her hands off him. As usual she was wearing a microbikini that covered absolutely nothing.

He stifled a groan of irritation as he forced a bright smile. "Hello, Lynette, is there something I can do for you?" He kept his tone strictly casual.

She batted her eyelashes and drawled, "Well, for starters you could ask me in."

Like hell he could. This little man-chaser was combustible, and he had no intention of fueling her fire. "I've got a better idea," he said as he sauntered past her and closed his door behind him. "I'll get some colas from the machine and we'll sit at one of the tables around the pool."

Damn it. That meant he wouldn't see Dinah when she came back, but he had to admit it wasn't really necessary that he do so. In spite of his misgivings about her, his longing for her had actually accelerated during her absence, and he'd been pacing around his room since noon watching for her.

Lynette's full lips formed into a pout. "Well, okay. Then will you go swimming with me?"

Todd shook his head as he put money in the soft drink machine. "Sorry, I get enough of that all week. I'd rather lounge around and watch others swim on weekends."

Dinah arrived home shortly after four and changed into red shorts and a red-and-white striped blouse. This time she wore a bra, but couldn't bring herself to put on shoes.

She loved the feel of the soft, thick carpet under her bare feet.

For a while she was busy unpacking and listening to messages on the answering machine, but all the time her thoughts were on Todd. Where was he? Was he still upset because of the way she'd treated him? Should she go over and ask him if there'd been any problems at the pool on Friday...?

Mentally she snapped her errant thoughts to attention. She was doing it again—making excuses to go to him, which was exactly what she didn't want to do. She'd never discourage him if she kept hanging around like a love-struck teenager.

Fifteen minutes later she slipped on her red sandals and headed across the street to the rec building after convincing herself that she needed to talk to some of the tenants to see if everything had gone smoothly while she was away. She figured that Todd probably wasn't even on the premises.

It was a hot sunny day, and the air-conditioned recreation building was packed with people—some playing cards, others reading or watching the ball game on a big-screen television. Even with the sliding glass doors closed and the constant hum of people talking, she could hear the noisy shouts and splashing of swimmers outside in the pool.

She was immediately greeted on all sides.

"Hey, Dinah, glad to see you back...."

"My kitchen sink's stopped up, and the plumber said he couldn't come till tomorrow...."

"The people next door have a new puppy that's cried for the last two nights...."

"The lifeguard says my Eddie can't swim in the pool for a week because he was ducking other kids, but he was only playing...."

Dinah sighed as she assured all and sundry that she'd look into their problems. Who was it that said everyone needs to be needed? She wished he could trade places with her for a day.

She finally made her way across the room and out onto the tiled deck. The pool was swarming with kids of all ages, and the part-time lifeguard had his hands full. He wasn't as good with youngsters as Todd was, but then few people were. He usually managed okay, though, just as he was doing now.

Dinah turned to stroll through the crowded area and caught sight of Todd sitting at one of the tables. He was facing her, but hadn't seen her because he was engrossed in conversation with a woman sitting across from him with her bare back to Dinah. She immediately recognized Lynette Patton, the underage sexy bombshell who had all the men in the complex lusting after her.

A sudden, swift wave of nausea made Dinah falter, and she gulped a deep breath of fresh air in an effort to fight it back. Not Todd, too! What a dunderhead she'd been to believe for a minute that she could compete with a seventeen-year-old nymphet.

While she'd been in Tucson missing him and chastizing herself for hurting him, he'd been happily seducing the local temptress!

While she was still battling the queasiness, Todd looked up and saw her. For a moment he looked startled—or was it guilty?—but then he smiled and stood. "Dinah, when did you get back?"

With a herculean effort she squared her shoulders and managed a tight little smile as she walked toward them.

"Hello, Todd, Lynette. You two look relaxed and content. Have you been swimming?"

Todd was dressed in his usual shorts and shirt, but Lynette was spilling out of the few scraps of material she was wearing. Dinah was tempted to send her home to put some clothes on, but knew such an action would be spite on her part rather than concern for public decency.

"Not yet," Lynette said in answer to Dinah's question. "Poor Todd gets so bored having to be in the pool all week that I didn't have the heart to make him feel he had to swim with me on his days off. We managed to find other things to do, didn't we?"

Todd blinked, and Dinah bit her lip to keep from crying. She'd had no idea he didn't like the job, and she didn't even want to think what those other things that they'd been doing might be.

"I didn't say that—" He glared at Lynette, but Dinah quickly interrupted.

"I'm sorry you're unhappy with the position, Todd." Her voice broke, and she paused before going on.

"Dinah, that's not what I said," he insisted. "I—"

"We . . . we'd hate to lose you," she continued, "but if you should decide to quit, I hope you'll give me time to find a replacement first."

She couldn't look at either of them and knew she had to get away fast. "If you'll excuse me, I've been gone, and I have a lot of catching up to do."

She turned and almost ran back into the building with Todd right at her heels. He followed her across the driveway and caught up with her at her front door. "Give me your key." It wasn't a request; it was a command.

She didn't want him to come in, but was too choked up to argue. He opened the door and accompanied her inside.

"Dinah, surely you're not going to believe anything that lying little brat tells you," he said.

She had her back to him and couldn't see his expression, but there was exasperation in his tone. "She came to my room and wanted me to let her in. No way was I going to be caught behind closed doors with her, so I suggested we sit outside by the pool. All I wanted was to get rid of her. When she suggested we go swimming, I told her I had enough of that during the week and wasn't in the mood. She put her own interpretation on it."

Dinah knew he was probably telling the truth. She'd seen how shamelessly Lynette flirted with him, but she'd never known him to encourage it. She also knew the girl's penchant for lying.

So pull yourself together, Dinah, and act like a relieved employer instead of a jealous lover.

Using all her acting skill, she turned and smiled at him. "I'm pleased to hear that, Todd. I'd hate to think you were unhappy working here, and as for Lynette...well... what you do on your own time is none of my business."

She thought she saw him wince before he glowered at her. "Oh, is that so?" His tone was broadly sarcastic. "Well, excuse me for thinking you might be just the tiniest bit upset to find me making time with a nude woman when you came back after being gone practically forever."

Dinah gasped. "She wasn't nude!"

"She might as well have been, and don't tell me you didn't notice," he answered angrily. "For that matter, what am I apologizing for anyway? It's your job to make the rules around here, so why don't you ban that sexy tease from the pool unless she's wearing at least a quarter of a yard of material? You're just asking for trouble if you don't.''

Dinah knew he was right, but she didn't appreciate him pointing out her shortcomings. ''If that is an official complaint, I'll make note of it and let you know how I plan to handle it,'' she said coldly. ''Now, if you'll excuse me, I have some calls to make. I'm sure you can find your way out.''

She walked away as the door slammed behind her.

Chapter Seven

At five-thirty on Monday afternoon, Todd walked into Orville Fischbeck's office suite with a mixture of anticipation and dread. The appraiser didn't know it, but it was possible that his report would shape the destiny of both Dinah and Todd.

Fischbeck, a little bald man with horn-rimmed glasses, greeted Todd and motioned him to sit down on the other side of the desk. "The collector who owns this egg is indeed fortunate," he said, happily displaying the article in his hand.

"Egg?" The only thing that word brought to mind was breakfast.

"Ah, yes. I knew it was a Fabergé egg as soon as I examined it, but I couldn't tell whether it was a copy or genuine."

Fabergé egg meant nothing to Todd. He'd never been especially interested in either jewelry or art, and this was his first insurance case.

"Umm . . . I'm afraid you have me at a disadvantage," he stammered, embarrassed at having to admit his ignorance. "My knowledge in this field is limited. Would you mind refreshing my memory?"

The appraiser smiled knowingly, and Todd squirmed. "Of course. Peter Carl Fabergé was court jeweler to the czars of Russia in the late-nineteenth and early-twentieth centuries. His clientele was worldwide, but he's best known for the jeweled Easter eggs he created for the czars. They, of course, are priceless now and unavailable, but this egg is definitely a product of the Fabergé workshops."

Todd felt anything but elated. Sick was a better way to describe the turmoil in his gut. "Then it's worth a couple of million dollars?" he asked, too upset to be discreet.

Fischbeck looked shocked. "Is that what the owner wants to insure it for? This isn't an original Fabergé design. It was probably made by one of his apprentices for a member of the worker's own family. Although the gold is valuable, there are no precious stones, and it's just a shell. There's no 'surprise.' "

Todd was too confused to care what the "surprise" was, but waited anxiously for the appraiser to continue. "An avid collector might pay up to one hundred thousand dollars for it if he had more money than sense, but two million? No way."

Todd's relief was only partial. Just because this little treasure was worth only a small portion of the full value of the missing jewels didn't exactly exonerate Dinah. Erhardt could have stolen it from somewhere else, and therefore it wouldn't be part of the gem theft, or it could represent only a portion of the investment of the money she would have gotten from the diamonds. If so, where was the rest?

A Fabergé egg had not been part of the inventory of the Erhardt's possessions taken at the time Anson was arrested, so where had it come from? If Dinah was totally innocent, where did she get the money to purchase such an expensive piece of art? And why did she keep it hidden away instead of displaying it proudly for all to see?

The tormenting questions echoed back and forth in his mind and gave him no peace.

Todd woke at five-thirty the following morning after a night of restless sleep. He was going to talk to Dinah this morning even if it meant he had to awaken her. He'd intended to corner her last night, but he'd been in too much of a quandary over what he'd learned about the Fabergé egg to attempt it. It would only have resulted in another quarrel.

Weren't there any clear-cut answers in this case? Why did everything have to be maybe this, or possibly that? He'd expected to know exactly where Dinah stood once he'd had the egg appraised. Instead he'd come away with even more uncertainties, and the whole thing was driving him out of his mind.

There was only one thing he knew for sure. He had to keep the lines of communication with Dinah open if he ever hoped to resolve this mess, and that meant controlling his raging emotions.

Dinah heard the buzz several times before she was awake enough to realize that it was the doorbell. Sleepily she rolled out of bed and groped for her white terry-cloth robe.

Darn, why did the tenants think it was perfectly acceptable to come to her with their complaints at any time of the day or night? Todd had been right. She was going to have to set some rules and adhere to them—not only about proper swimming attire, which she'd already attended to, but about her own working hours, as well. She was still upset by the scene with him, and it was affecting her ability to fall asleep.

Tying the robe around her, she stumbled to the door and opened it. Todd, fully clothed in jeans and a shirt, stood on the other side of the screen, looking apologetic. "I'm sorry to wake you, honey, but I couldn't sleep. I need to talk to you. May I come in?"

How could she deny him anything when he asked so poignantly? She ran one hand through her tousled hair and unlocked the screen with the other, then stood back to let him in. "Is something wrong?" she asked anxiously.

"Yes, something's wrong." His gaze roamed lovingly over her from her sleep-swollen face down to her bare feet and up again, making her quiver with the need for his touch.

"I can't seem to function when you're ignoring me," he continued, then reached out and took her in his arms.

She didn't struggle. She couldn't. Not when he was holding her so gently and rubbing her cheek with his own.

With a contented sigh she put her arms around his waist, and for a long time they just stood there silently holding each other. His familiar scent filled her nostrils, and even at this hour of the morning his face was smoothly shaven. A small thoughtfulness on his part, but so very endearing.

When Todd finally moved, it was to unknot her sash and put his arms underneath her robe, cuddling her soft, willing body, protected only by a short cotton nightie, against his firm strength. His hand slid down her hip to the bareness of her thigh, then up again, underneath the gown, to rest on her buttocks.

Even as her unruly body snuggled against him, her good sense fought to assert itself. "Oh, Todd," she breathed, hating what she must do. "Please. No."

He raised his head and looked at her, a small wry grin tugging at the corners of his mouth. "Please *no?* Sweetheart, please is supposed to mean *yes.*"

Even though he was teasing, his voice was husky with wanting.

She closed her eyes and hid her face in his shoulder. "See what you do to me?" she scolded tenderly. "You tear me apart with conflicting emotions. I want so badly to say yes, but we both know that type of relationship between us would only end in heartbreak. We have nothing in common but overactive libidos."

"And what's wrong with overactive libidos? I guarantee you that the next few hours could be sheer heaven for both of us."

She finally found the strength to straighten up and face him again. "I don't doubt that for a minute," she said grimly, "but I'm not willing to face the hell that would come afterward. I've been through that once, and once was enough."

For a moment Todd's arms tightened around her, and his expression was hard, angry. "What did that bastard you married do to you, Dinah?" he demanded. "Tell me."

It seemed to her that there was a note of pleading in his last two words, but she couldn't discuss Anson with him. She couldn't discuss Anson with anybody.

"That was a long time ago. It doesn't matter anymore," she said, but knew that it did.

If only she could talk about it with Todd. She needed to share her doubts and fears with him, but he wouldn't understand. Only her family and Bernie and Sarah Rose believed unconditionally that she knew nothing of Anson's larcenous activities until he was caught and exposed. No one else, neither her friends, nor the authorities nor the news media had believed that she could have been so unaware, so innocent, so stupid.

When she divorced him and moved to Phoenix, she'd put all that behind her. No one here knew about her past, and she intended to keep it that way.

Gently but firmly she pulled away from Todd. "Before we got sidetracked you said you wanted to discuss something with me," she said, totally changing the subject. "Why don't you make the coffee while I get dressed, and we can have breakfast while we talk?"

By the time she was dressed and ready to face the day, Todd had the coffee made and a pot of something bubbling on the stove. She lifted the lid and sniffed. "Oatmeal?" she asked. "I only use that to hold my meat loaf together."

Todd was buttering toast. "It's good for you," he informed her. "Eggs and bacon are filled with cholesterol, but oatmeal and low-fat milk provide protein and fiber. It'll put roses in your cheeks."

"Thank you, I think," she said doubtfully as she took two bowls from the cupboard and spooned hot cereal into them.

While they ate, the tenor of their conversation changed. It was Todd who set the tone. "Did you believe me when I told you I have no interest in Lynette Patton?" he asked.

Dinah smiled at him reassuringly. "Of course I did. I know what a pest she can be, and you'll be happy to know that I had a talk with her mother yesterday. She won't be showing up around the pool in that string bikini again, and to make sure, I'm having signs printed regarding proper swimming attire, which will be posted for all to see."

He put his hand over hers where it lay on the table. "I appreciate that. It will make my job more manageable if she's toned down a little. It's easier to light fires in teenage boys than it is to put them out, and if she doesn't bank her incendiary tendencies, it won't be long before she, or more likely the poor kid she's igniting, gets burned."

He removed his hand from hers and took a swallow of his coffee, then put the mug down and looked at her. "Now, tell me why you've been giving me the brush-off for the past week."

His tone was gentle, but she could hear the steely determination behind it and knew it would do no good to spar with him. "You know, Todd, you and Lynette have a lot in common," she said. "You both tend to light fires without giving proper thought to the consequences."

Todd's brown eyes opened wide. "That's not true," he protested. "I don't—"

"Yes you do," she insisted. "Unlike Lynette, you don't do it indiscriminately just to test your ability, but I'd be willing to bet that when you were her age you did."

"Damn it, Dinah, I did no such thing," he roared, obviously protesting too vigorously.

"Of course you did," she said with a grin, "and I'll bet you had to beat the girls off with a stick."

A suspicious sparkle lit his eyes. "Oh, I couldn't admit to that," he drawled. "Brush them out of my bath with a broom, possibly, but..." He shrugged. "What can I say?"

They both laughed, but Dinah was the first to sober. "You see what I mean. You were probably an adorable baby, an appealing toddler, a cute preadolescent and the sexiest hunk in school from junior high through college. You know exactly how to charm a woman, and you use that skill to get almost anything you want."

Todd's amused smile turned to a frown. "I'm not sure whether you're flattering me or insulting me," he said coolly. "You've indicated before that you thought I was little better than an alley cat on the prowl—"

"Oh, Todd, no. That's not at all what I mean. You're probably the nicest man I've ever known. That's why I find it so hard to resist you. You're everything I ever wanted in a lover, but . . ."

"But what?" He sounded perplexed. "Why are you afraid to let me get close to you?"

"Because for you it's a game." He opened his mouth to protest, but she hurried on. "Or at best, a pleasant diversion until school starts and you have better things to occupy your time, but I don't do recreational sex."

He looked as shocked as if she'd slapped him, and she knew she'd blundered again. "Please, Todd, I'm not putting you down. I'm just saying that we have different sets of values. I need commitment in a relationship."

"Why are you so sure that I'm not capable of making a commitment?" he asked quietly.

She shook her head and sighed. "I'm doing this badly," she apologized. "I don't doubt but that you're capable of making a commitment when the right woman comes along, but that woman isn't me and we both know it. You aren't ready to marry and settle down, and when you are, it will be with someone your own age. Possibly someone you'll meet in law school."

It was a long moment before he answered. "Is that what you want? Marriage?"

She stirred her cooling cereal. "I'm not looking for a husband, but, yes, eventually I'd like to marry again. I don't want to spend the rest of my life alone, and if possible, I'd like to have children."

Her mouth snapped shut, but it was already too late. She hadn't intended to mention children.

"Why didn't you have them with Erhardt?"

The question jolted Dinah. Not only because he'd asked it but also because she no longer used the name Erhardt, and she was almost certain she'd never told him Anson's last name. She'd never told anyone in Phoenix. The people who knew she was divorced just assumed that Swensen was her married name instead of the one she'd been born with.

"I...I...that is, we..." she stammered.

Oh, for God's sake, answer the man, Dinah. It's a natural question after you brought up the subject. If you'd learn to think before you speak, you wouldn't get into these situations. Obviously you slipped up at some time and mentioned Anson's last name, too.

"We wanted a baby, but I couldn't get pregnant," she blurted, and hoped he'd let it go at that.

He didn't. "Do you know which of you was infertile?"

She shook her head. "Neither one, actually. We had all the tests and there was nothing wrong with either of us. I wouldn't marry again just to have children, but if it happened, I'd be very pleased."

"You and I could make beautiful babies," he said softly, almost as though he'd spoken his thoughts inadvertently.

Hearing him say it was almost more than Dinah could bear. "Stop it, Todd," she said angrily as she pushed back her chair and stood. "You haven't been listening to a word I've said."

She walked over to the sink and stood looking out the window. "I'd hoped it wouldn't come to this, but I guess it was inevitable. I'm giving you notice. Start looking for another job because in two weeks I'll have a new lifeguard to take your place."

Although she had her back to him she heard his chair topple over as he jumped up. She gripped the edge of the sink as he came to stand beside her. "Are you firing me, Dinah?"

She took a deep breath. "I prefer to think of it as a strong suggestion that you quit. Naturally I'll give you a glowing reference—you're an excellent lifeguard, but we simply can't work together any longer. Surely you can see that."

Todd had been dealt a blow, and he was reeling. Dinah was throwing him out! Oh, she dressed it up with pretty terms and compliments, but all the same she was telling him to get out of her life.

Why was he so surprised? He knew he'd been pushing her, letting his need to touch her, hold her, overrule his caution. Asking probing questions that he knew she didn't want to answer, and breaching his professionalism by falling in love with her.

He hunched over, trying to deflect the second blow, but it was no use. It landed with stunning force. *Falling in love with her.* Of course he was in love with Dinah. Why had it taken him so long to recognize it?

No other woman had ever had the impact on him that she did. He'd been bowled over right from the start, but at first he'd thought it was just physical.

It had been that, all right. He'd had all the male reactions to prove it, but as the days went by, he should have realized what was happening.

Now it was too late. He was trapped in a love that was too compelling to deny, and too impossible to admit!

He got a firm grip on his turbulent emotions and turned to look at her. If he truly loved her, and he knew he did, then he'd let her go now before they got any further involved. It was the one decent thing he could do for her.

"I guess you're right," he said, and silently cursed the quaver in his voice. "I'd appreciate it if you'd let me stay for the next two weeks, but I'll leave then. I suppose you want me to vacate my room, too?"

She didn't speak, just nodded.

"Can we be friends until then?"

Again she nodded, and he knew it was time to get out of there. "I want you to know that you'll always be very dear to me," he said, and strode to the door, closing it softly behind him.

For the rest of the week Dinah studiously avoided Todd. She stayed away from the pool and the rec building, and spent more time than usual at her other properties, seeing to minor repairs and listening to tenant complaints. No matter how hard she tried to please, there was always a hard-core group in any apartment building that was never satisfied.

She was almost grateful to them now because they kept her mind and body busy and offered a welcome, though brief, respite from her grief over Todd's imminent departure. Dinah had never known grief before. Her experience with Anson she'd described as shock, disillusionment, anger, but not grief.

She'd always thought you grieved when someone close to you died, and of course you did, but the loss she'd felt after she'd dismissed Todd was very much akin to a death—the death of hope, of happiness, of a joyful future.

How could she have fallen so deeply in love with him so quickly?

Her date with Jeff Marshall on Tuesday had been just short of a disaster. He'd taken her to an expensive restaurant, then a movie and finally a jazz bar for a nightcap.

He'd been the perfect escort, but she'd merely walked through the experience, trying to remember to laugh, talk or sit quietly at all the right times. Her mind and heart had been with Todd, so much so that one time she was sure she saw him mirrored in one of the store windows, but when she'd looked again, he wasn't there.

She'd decided then that she was going to have to get a grip on herself, and she'd managed to get through the evening without any more hallucinations.

She must have done a fair job of hiding her disinterest because Jeff had invited her to spend Sunday with him in Apache Junction. She'd declined, inventing a previous engagement, but when he extended the invitation to the following Sunday, she changed her mind and accepted. That was the weekend Todd would be moving out, and she couldn't stand to be there when he did. Besides, it was time for her to put him behind her and get on with her life.

Maybe if she went through the empty motions long enough, they'd begin to have meaning again.

By Monday the strain was becoming unbearable. Although Dinah and Todd had agreed to remain friends, they both knew that was impossible, and Dinah had seen him only a couple of times when she'd had to go to the pool or the rec building on business. Even then they hadn't spoken but had merely waved politely.

Dinah was sleeping badly, her appetite was nonexistent and her temper was short. She'd called the employment agency about a new lifeguard, but so far there'd been only two applicants, and neither was suitable.

How could anyone measure up to Todd?

It was three o'clock in the afternoon, and she was on the phone, trying to placate a woman whose lease wasn't being renewed because her last child was now eighteen.

"But surely you could make an exception in my case," the woman wailed. "We've been here ever since the place opened. It's our home!"

"I know," Dinah said soothingly, "but the terms of your lease are explicit. You have to have a youngster under the age of eighteen to stay here. Besides, now that your daughter will be going away to college, think of how nice it will be to live somewhere that's quiet and not overrun with kids. I'll be happy to help you find something—"

She was interrupted by someone shouting her name, and looked out the window to see a woman running across the driveway from the direction of the pool. By the time she'd hastily terminated her conversation and put down the phone, the woman was banging on her door.

"Dinah! Dinah! Come quick. There's been a fight! An accident. Todd—"

The world stopped turning for Dinah as she tore open the door and almost banged the woman with the screen as she dashed out of the house and down the walk.

Oh my God, Todd. An accident.

She didn't waste time asking what happened but sprinted across the street to the pool area, the other woman right behind her. As she ran through the gate, she saw a crowd of people gathered at the far side of the pool.

"Be careful," the woman called. "It's slippery. You don't want to fall, too."

The words flew right past Dinah without registering as she elbowed her way through the crowd.

At the centre Todd lay crumpled on the tile, unconscious, a dark red pool forming under his head.

Dinah fought the waves of panic that threatened to overwhelm her as she dropped to her knees beside the still figure. "Todd," she said, frantically reaching out to touch his white face. "Oh, Todd, darling, open your eyes and look at me."

There was no response, and she moved her hand carefully across his cheek and down to the back of his neck. She felt a warm, sticky liquid, and her fingers came away bloody.

Her heart pounded with alarm, and a whimper escaped from her throat, but she steeled herself to remain calm. "Call 9-1-1," she ordered in a voice taut with anxiety. "Tell them to send an ambulance and the police."

She hadn't been speaking to anyone in particular, but knew her orders would be carried out. She wanted to put Todd's head in her lap but knew better than to move it until the extent of the injury was known. Instead, she took his hand and held it lovingly between both of hers.

It was only then that she became aware of the figure huddled at his other side and sobbing. It was Lynette Patton, and she was once more practically nude in that forbidden bikini.

Rage diluted Dinah's panic. "I should have known you'd have something to do with this," she flared bitterly.

"I didn't. I swear I didn't," Lynette wailed. "Slash didn't mean to hurt Todd. Honest, it was an accident." Tears streamed from her red-rimmed eyes.

"Who's Slash?" Dinah demanded.

"He...he's a guy I've been goin' out with. Kind of, you know, the jealous type, but . . ."

A commotion among the spectators diverted Dinah's attention, and she saw the security guard pushing his way through to her. "What's going on?"

"I'm not sure," she told him, "but an ambulance should be here any minute. I want you to call the property-management firm and tell them to get someone over immediately, then question these people and find out ex-actly what happened. Take it down in writing.''

He darted off in search of a phone, and a siren sounded in the distance as she turned her attention back to Lynette. ''As for you,'' she said, her tone cold and deadly, ''go home and start packing, because I'm giving you and your family until the end of the week to get out of here.''

Lynette gasped. ''You can't do that!'' Her face was twisted with shock.

''Just watch me.''

A moan from Todd drove everything else from Dinah's mind, and she turned her head to look at him. His eyes were open but not quite focused. ''Dinah?'' he asked.

Giddy with relief, she squeezed the hand she was hold-ing. ''I'm right here, sweetheart.''

With an effort he managed to focus his gaze on her. ''What's all the noise, and who's pounding me on the head?'' His voice was whispery and unsteady.

The noise was the sirens from the ambulance and police car that drove up just outside the area and screeched to a stop.

She continued to hold his hand with one of hers, and with the other she stroked the side of his head. ''The paramedics and the police just arrived. You've been in-jured. How do you feel?''

Before he could answer, two white-coated men arrived with a black bag and a stretcher. ''What happened?'' one of them asked as the other immediately started to exam-ine him.

''I'm not sure,'' Todd answered, ''but my head feels like something exploded inside it.''

''I wasn't here, and he's been unconscious until a cou-ple of minutes ago,'' Dinah explained. She looked around for Lynette, but she'd apparently taken off when the police arrived.

A tall, dark-haired man standing nearby volunteered the information. His name was Youngman, and he and his family were valued tenants.

"There was a scuffle between Todd and a guy I'd never seen before," he said. "A biker type, all dressed in black, who was with Lynette Patton. I don't know what it was about, but Todd had him by the scruff of the neck and was evicting him when the guy kicked his foot back and tripped Todd. If Todd had gone over the side forward he'd have been okay, but he tried to right himself and fell backward, hitting the back of his head on the side of the pool as he fell in. The biker took off, but several of us dived in and pulled Todd out. He was unconscious, but I don't think he'd breathed any water into his lungs."

"Hey, thanks, fella," Todd said, his voice raspy.

"Yes, Mr. Youngman, thank you," Dinah added. "Will you please tell the police what you told me?"

The man nodded and walked away.

A few minutes later, the paramedics put Todd on the stretcher. He protested. "I don't need to go to the hospital. It's just a headache. A Band-Aid and an aspirin will take care of it."

"Better have some X rays," advised one of the medics. "You seem okay, but it's always best to be sure."

They loaded him into the ambulance, and Dinah started to climb in with him. One of the attendants stopped her. "Are you a relative?"

She glared at him, set to do battle if necessary. "I'm his mother," she said in a tone that dared him to challenge her.

He laughed and waved her inside. "If you say so," he said, and laughed again as he closed the doors.

Dinah sat down beside the stretcher and took Todd's hand. He squeezed her hand and grinned. "Hi, Ma. Do you think it would shock the medics if you kissed me?"

"If it does, that's their problem," she murmured as she leaned over him and covered his mouth with hers.

It was a tender blending of lips. An expression of caring that went beyond passion to a melding of their spirits. Todd sighed and murmured, "Don't leave me," then closed his eyes but continued to clutch her hand.

"I have no intention of leaving you," she promised as her lips caressed his eyelids, then brushed down his cheek to nibble at first one corner of his mouth and then the other.

He shivered. "Oh, God, I love it when you do that."

"I love it when I do that, too," she confessed. "You're so delightfully kissable. When you're feeling better I'll show you more of my talents."

He opened his eyes and looked straight into hers. "Promise?"

"I promise," she said without blinking.

He whispered something unintelligible that sounded like "I love you" but it was so soft and garbled that she couldn't trust her interpretation. Just because that's what she wanted so badly to hear didn't make it so. He was probably just repeating that he loved what she did to him, and that was a different matter altogether.

At the hospital Todd was examined, X rayed and released with instructions to see a doctor in a couple of days, or earlier if he started seeing double or had any other unusual symptoms.

By the time Dinah had gotten his prescription for pain medication filled at the hospital pharmacy and called for a cab, the sun was down and it was getting dark. A nurse insisted on wheeling Todd out to the curb in a wheelchair and helping him into the taxi. Dinah got in beside him and gave the driver her address.

When they drove up in front of her apartment, she told Todd to wait in the cab, then hurried into the house and got her purse. After paying the fare, she put her arm around Todd, who was still dizzy, and helped him to walk. Her front door stood wide open as she'd left it when she'd run out hours before, but nothing inside had been disturbed.

They were across the living room and into the hall before Todd spoke. "Where are you taking me?"

"To the bedroom," she said. "I'm going to put you to bed, and then fix you something to eat. It's long past dinnertime."

They turned left and went a few steps down the hall to her room. "You mean you're going to let me sleep with you?" he asked, his tone betraying his surprise.

She smiled and sat him down on the bottom of the bed. "I mean you're going to sleep here, and I'm going to bunk on the couch."

He looked disappointed. "Oh. In that case I'd better go to my own room. I'll be all right."

She turned down the covers and fluffed up the pillows, then sat down beside him. "I'd really like for you to stay tonight, Todd," she said carefully. "I'll worry if you insist on staying over there by yourself. I know the doctor said there was no fracture or concussion, but a head injury can be tricky. Please humor me."

With a groan he reached for her and pulled her against him. "You don't have to plead with me to spend the night with you, sweetheart, even if it is in separate beds. I'm grateful for your thoughtfulness. I just don't want to be a bother."

What was there about this man that was so irresistible? It wasn't just his looks. Right now he was pale and drawn with dark shadows under his pain-dimmed eyes, but still she couldn't resist him. All he had to do was hold out his arms to her and she'd come to him.

She leaned into his embrace and touched her forehead to his. "You could never be a bother. Now come get into bed before you collapse."

He kissed her lingeringly before he released her and stood up. "Do you mind if I take a shower first?" he asked. "I feel so grimy and sweaty."

"Are you sure you can manage by yourself?" Her tone betrayed her misgivings. "If you're still dizzy..."

"It's not as bad now," he assured her. "I'll be all right, and I'll feel better once I'm clean again."

"Well, if you're sure, but don't get your bandage wet. While you're doing that, I'll heat up a can of soup. Do you need clean clothes? I could go across the driveway and get your pajamas."

He put his fingers under her chin and lifted her face to look at him. "I don't wear pajamas," he said with a wicked grin.

Her eyes widened. The picture that confession brought to mind made her blush. "Oh."

He hugged her. "Don't worry, I won't embarrass you. My trunks are dry. I'll wear them to bed."

Forty-five minutes later, Todd had finished his shower, they'd eaten their soup and she'd tucked him into her double-size bed. "Are you comfortable?" she asked anxiously as she pulled the sheet over him.

He smiled. "As comfortable as I can be with a knot at the base of my skull."

She had a compelling desire to relieve his pain. "Would you like an ice bag? I can't give you another pill for two more hours."

"Sweetheart, I'm fine. All I need is a good-night kiss."

She sat down on the edge of the bed and leaned over to oblige. He put his arms around her and pulled her close as his mouth opened in invitation. Slowly she rimmed his lips with her tongue before accepting the moist intimacy of his unspoken request.

"We'll save more of that for another time," she said as she raised her head a few seconds later and looked down at him. "You need some rest and I need a shower. If the phone rings while I'm in the bathroom, just ignore it. The machine will answer it."

He still held her. "Will you come back when you're finished and give me another kiss?" His tone was husky.

She reached up to turn off the lamp beside the bed. "If you're still awake," she promised.

"Leave the light on," he said as he released her. "I'll be awake."

Dinah's shower was quick but refreshing. A reaction to the shocking events of the past few hours was beginning to set in, and she was tired to the point of exhaustion. It felt good to stand under the stinging hot water and let it soak the tension out of her weary body.

After brushing her teeth, she put on a clean white cotton nightgown with ruffles at the low square neckline and the hem, then turned out the light and walked barefoot down the hall to check on Todd.

He was lying with his face turned toward the door, watching for her. He uttered a murmur of approval when she appeared, and held out his arms to her. She turned off the lamp and sank into them, and he pulled her down to lay full-length beside him.

She didn't even think about resisting when this time he initiated the kiss. It was gentle but filled with longing, and she snuggled against him and caressed his back and shoulders.

"Stay with me, Dinah." His voice was ragged. "I promise I won't make a pass. To tell the truth, I don't feel good enough for anything strenuous. I just want to hold you, to sleep next to you, to know you care enough to want to be with me."

His words sent shivers of pure happiness through her, and she put her fingers to his lips. "It's all right, darling," she said shakily. "I won't leave you. I told you that earlier today. I'd like very much to sleep with you."

His arms tightened around her, and he nuzzled the damp pulse at the side of her neck. "I don't just want you with me, Dinah," he whispered. "I *need* you with me, and I don't think I'm ever going to be whole again without you."

Chapter Eight

Todd drifted up from the depths of sleep with a dull ache in his head. When he opened his eyes, there was sunlight streaming through the window of an unfamiliar room, and for a moment he had no idea where he was.

Then he remembered. Dinah! Good Lord, how could he have forgotten?

He turned onto his side, eager to take her in his arms again, but the sudden movement sent shock waves of pain pounding through his head and shoulders. With a moan he fell back and lay quietly until the anguish subsided.

There was no hurry. Dinah's side of the bed was empty.

The door was closed, but he could hear her talking to somebody. Since there was no answer, he assumed she was on the telephone. A glance at the bedside clock told him it was ten minutes after nine.

Damn, he never slept that late. She must have been up for at least a couple of hours, probably longer. What about the pool? They couldn't open it without a lifeguard, and

Todd knew he'd be lucky if he could get out of bed. He was in no shape to be responsible for the safety of the swimmers.

He lay there listening to the intermittent sound of Dinah's warm, sweet voice. It was like a lullaby—soothing, relaxing, reminding him of how soft and comforting she'd felt last night when she'd curled up against him in sleep. If he hadn't slept so soundly and had wakened when she started to get up, he'd have convinced her to stay in bed with him.

He cursed the stirring in his loins. No, it was better this way. If just thinking about her could arouse him, even as rotten as he was feeling this morning, he wouldn't have had a prayer of resisting the powerful urge to make love to her if she was willing.

He couldn't do that and retain even a modicum of self-respect until he was off this case, and he could no longer trust his self-control. It was time to confess his indiscretion to Wes and ask to be replaced.

Even then he'd have to leave her and go back to Los Angeles until the case was resolved, but there was one thing he knew for sure. If it turned out she was guilty, he'd still want to marry her.

Carefully, so as not to set off the explosions in his head again, he pushed himself up and sat on the side of the bed. He was hunched over with his elbows on his knees and his head in his hands when he heard the door open softly, and the scent of apple blossoms preceded Dinah into the room.

"Oh, Todd," she said. "You shouldn't try to get up. Your head still hurts, doesn't it?"

She knelt between his legs, and he pulled her close and buried his face in her silky hair. She put her arms around his waist, her cheek against his bare chest, and all his good intentions melted.

He knew there wasn't a chance in hell that he could leave her, even for her own good. He wasn't even sure he could resist the terrible need to pull her back into bed, remove the pretty peach-colored dress she was wearing, and spend the day assuaging the pent-up longing that had been tormenting him for so long.

She moved her cheek up his chest and kissed the hollow at his throat. His hands trembled as they tangled in her long golden hair. "You'd better lie back down, and I'll bring you breakfast," she murmured as she trailed kisses along his collarbone.

He stifled a moan and gritted his teeth as he called on what was left of his resolve and strength to break their embrace and move her back so he could stand up. "I'm much better this morning," he lied as his head swam and his vision blurred. "I'll have coffee with you, but then I'm going home to get dressed. What are you doing for a lifeguard?"

"I've closed the pool for the day shift until you feel well enough to work again," she said. "The evening guard will open it when he comes to work at five."

Forty-five minutes later Todd unlocked the door and let himself into his room. Dinah had insisted that he eat breakfast and take another pain pill, and now he felt better, stronger and more clear-headed.

He rummaged around, gathering up clean clothes and putting them on. It wasn't until he was lacing his Reeboks that he noticed the flashing red light on his telephone answering machine. Getting up, he went over to the desk, rewound the tape and set the switch on Play, then sat down to listen to his messages.

The first one was a computer trying to get him to subscribe to a magazine. The second was a coded message from his firm in Los Angeles. It was Wes's voice saying,

"Hi, Todd, this is Uncle Wes. Call me when you get in."
It was set up to alert Todd that he was to call the home office, but to not give away his cover in case someone besides Todd listened to it. The third was the same message,
and the fourth was Lynette Patton pleading with him to
call her as soon as he got home from the hospital.

After that there were four more from Wes, each more
profane and urgent. The gist of the last one was "I've been
trying since one-thirty yesterday afternoon to get you, and
here it is Tuesday morning and you're still not there. For
God's sake, quit messing around and call me!"

Wes's urgency communicated itself to Todd, and with a
feeling of dread he dialed his boss's number.

The phone was answered on the first ring. "Wes, it's
me," Todd said. "I—"

"Where in hell have you been?" the other man practically exploded into the line, demanding to know why Todd
hadn't answered his messages but never giving him a
chance to explain.

Finally, when he began to accuse Todd of playing
around and not doing his job, Todd yelled right back at
him. "Shut up a minute and listen, damn it! There was an
accident and I've been in the hospital. I just got your messages."

There was a welcome silence at the other end of the line
before Wes spoke again, this time quietly. "Accident?
Hospital? What happened? Are you all right?"

Todd recounted the story, leaving out the part about him
spending the night with Dinah. He didn't actually say that
he'd been kept in the hospital all night, but when Wes assumed that to be the case, Todd didn't correct him, either.

"I've got a bump on the back of my head that aches,
and I'm still a little woozy, but I'll be fine," he said in

conclusion. "Now, tell me what's happened back there that's so important it couldn't wait?"

"Oh, I'll tell you, all right," Wes said gruffly. "I just hope it's not too late."

Todd didn't feel like playing games, and he'd had about all of his overbearing boss that he could stand. "Too late for what? Good God, Wes, if you don't tell me what's wrong, how do you expect me to—?"

"Anson Erhardt's out."

Todd felt as if he'd been hit in the stomach. "Out? You mean his parole had been granted and he'll be *getting* out, don't you?"

"I mean he's out of prison and gone." For the first time since Todd had known him, Wesley Nelson sounded defeated.

Todd closed his eyes and wished his head would stop spinning. "What happened?"

"Our man on the case went on a week-long drunk and missed the fact that the hearing had been moved up a few days." Wes's tone was thick with disgust. "When we didn't hear from him for a while, we started calling him, but his wife kept insisting that he was working and she didn't know when he'd be home. By the time we found out that he wasn't on the job, Erhardt had been paroled and released. The justice system won't give out any information about their parolees, and we can't find him."

Todd understood now why Wes had been so frantic when he couldn't locate Todd, either, and he could almost feel sorry for his boss. The insurance company was one of the firm's biggest clients, and they weren't going to like this at all.

"He hasn't been here to see his ex-wife," Todd said.

"How can you be sure? You've been in the hospital since yesterday afternoon," Wes reminded him.

"I know, but Dinah was with me."

"All night?" Wes sounded a tad more hopeful.

Todd paused, then reluctantly gave in. "Yes, all night. She went to the hospital with me, and after I was treated and released, she took me to her place. I just came from her, and while I've been talking to you I've been watching the front of her apartment from my window. Erhardt hasn't been here."

If Wes had made a suggestive remark, Todd would have told him exactly what he could do with his case, but for once the other man had the good sense to let it ride.

"Look, I'm sorry you were injured," he said. "As soon as you feel up to it, fax me a report. Meanwhile, are you able to work? Do you need help?"

"I'm not steady enough to work today, but I'll probably be okay by tomorrow. You're the one who's always telling me I'm a hardheaded son of a gun, and you've just been proven right."

Wes chuckled. "I think I put it more succinctly than that, but don't push your luck. If you need a backup, get one."

"I will," Todd assured him. "If I do, I'll use the same operative I hired to tail Dinah last weekend when she went out of town. Don't worry, if Erhardt shows up, I'm not going to lose him."

Todd spent the rest of the morning sitting in the comfortable chair that he'd pulled up in front of the window and watching the people and cars that came and went on the street. By one o'clock he was fighting the urge to sleep and realized that the pain pills must be making him drowsy.

He got up and went outside, hoping a short walk in the fresh air would wake him up, and was just in time to meet

Dinah coming across the street. She was carrying a covered platter and his bottle of medication.

"Hi," she said with a bright smile. "I was just coming over to check on you and bring the tablets you forgot to take with you when you left. I also fixed you some turkey sandwiches."

She seemed so open and caring that he wanted to hug her right there on the street for everyone to see, but how could he be sure her concern was real and not just a cover-up to disguise the possibility that she was waiting to turn a fortune in stolen gems over to her recently paroled ex-husband?

He managed an answering smile. "Thanks. Come on in and share the sandwiches with me."

He put an arm around her shoulders and led her into the recreation building. If she was with him, he could relax and not be afraid he'd miss something.

He stopped in front of the vending machine and searched in his pockets for change. "I'll get the colas," he said, and began feeding quarters into it.

Back in his room he steered clear of the bed and rearranged the upholstered chair and the one from the desk so they could sit next to each other.

Once he'd managed to convince her that he felt much better and would be able to go to work in a day or two, she asked him what had caused the disturbance at the pool.

He swallowed the bite of sandwich he'd been chewing. "It was another case of Lynette Patton showing off. Apparently she'd told that Neanderthal she was with that I'd been hitting on her, and he came storming down to the pool, snorting fire and smoke. I told him to shut up and leave before I tossed him out, and he threw a punch at me. I deflected it and was evicting him when he tripped me."

Dinah sighed. "Well, Lynette won't be bothering you anymore after Friday. I gave her mother until then to move out." She shook her head. "I feel sorry for the poor woman. Her husband left her when Lynette was little, and she's totally incompetent when it comes to handling the girl. I've suggested family counseling, but that's all I can do."

Todd reached over and took her hand. "You can't shoulder the problems of all your tenants, love."

For a moment they sat in silence, then Dinah got up and dropped a quick kiss on the top of his head. "I've got work to do," she said, "and you need some rest, so I'll run along."

She went to the desk and picked up the plastic prescription bottle, took off the lid and shook two pills into the palm of her hand. "Here," she said, and handed them to him. "Take these and lie down."

He put one in his mouth, but closed his fist over the other, then took a mouthful of cola and swallowed. "Yes, ma'am," he said with a grin. "Now do I get a proper goodbye kiss?"

He stood and took her in his arms.

Twenty minutes later he was still tingling from that last kiss when a white Camaro drove up in front of Dinah's apartment and stopped at the curb. The driver's side was closest to Todd, and when a man dressed in a blue suit got out, Todd didn't need his binoculars to recognize him.

His image was burned into Todd's mind.

It was Dinah's ex-husband, Anson Erhardt.

A bouncy song from Madonna's newest album provided background music as Dinah assembled the ingredients for the cookies she was going to bake. She sang along with it, faking the words she didn't know and tapping her long wooden spoon against the metal bowl in time with the beat. It was such a relief to be happy again!

Todd wanted her, and all was right with her world.

Oh, she knew it wasn't that simple. There were still a lot of reasons why a relationship between them would never work, but she wasn't going to think about that now. After sleeping cuddled in his arms last night, she knew she wasn't going to fight her feelings any longer.

For the first time in years she felt totally alive again, and she was going to cherish every minute while it lasted and forget about the future. Whatever was going to happen would happen, and she'd deal with it then.

The future caught up with her five minutes later when the doorbell rang.

She danced a happy jig all the way to the door, then opened it and froze. She hadn't seen the man on the other side of the screen for five years, and he was supposed to be locked up in a California prison, but he still looked exactly as he had when they were married and living together.

She clutched the knob and tried to catch her breath.

"Hello, Dinah," he said softly.

She swallowed and cleared her throat. "H-hello, Anson." Her voice was barely above a whisper. "Wh-what are you doing here?"

"I came to see you. May I come in?"

He sounded so normal, as if he were greeting a friend he hadn't seen for a few days, not a wife who'd divorced him years ago and run away.

"Y-yes, of course." She knew she was stammering, but she couldn't seem to get her thoughts in order.

For a moment they both just stood there until Anson spoke again. "Would you mind unlocking the door?"

Dinah, you idiot, pull yourself together and stop acting like a slow-witted child. It's not as if you didn't know he was coming up for parole. You'd better take charge of this situation or he will.

She unlocked the door, then pushed it open to let him in. "I'm sorry," she said, and was pleased to find that she'd finally gotten control of her voice, "but I was shocked. You were the last person I expected to see."

Now that there was no screen between them, she realized that he had changed a little. He looked older. There were lines in his face that hadn't been there before, and there was a trace of white sprinkled in his dark brown hair.

He frowned. "Didn't you know I was coming up for parole?"

"Yes, Bernie told me when he stopped by on his way through Phoenix a couple of weeks ago, but I didn't think you knew where I was."

A thought occurred to her. "He told you, didn't he?"

He reached out and ran his hand down her smooth unbound hair. "I've always known where you were, Dinah. Did you honestly think I'd lose track of you?"

She backed away, dislodging his hand, and walked ahead of him into the living room. "Sit down," she said, motioning to the sofa. "Can I get you something to drink?"

Now she was doing it, acting as if he were a casual friend instead of the man she'd slept with for seven years. She realized that her knees were shaking, and she abruptly sat down in the chair.

"Maybe later," he said. "I didn't mean to upset you. I should have phoned, but I...I guess I was afraid you'd say you didn't want to see me."

She was almost glad to hear the catch in his voice. It meant that he wasn't as composed as he pretended to be.

"Anson..."

What could she say to him? *You're right, I didn't want to see you.* That would be cruel after he'd spent so many years locked behind bars. She'd been his wife, for heaven's sake. The least she could do was be kind to him. She surely owed him that much.

She tried again. "I'm glad you were released," she said cautiously, forming her words in her mind before she spoke. "I hated the thought of you being locked up like that."

"Did you really?" He sounded as if he were surprised.

"Of course, but that doesn't mean I approve of what you did, or that I could ever...um...be close to you again."

He said nothing, and she wished he'd stayed away and not put them through this.

"I have a new life, now, and I like it," she continued. "I've learned to take care of myself and not depend on anyone. It's a good feeling."

"I could have taken care of you while I was in prison if you had let me," he told her, and she knew he was referring to the fortune in gems he had hidden away somewhere.

"I want nothing to do with that," she said angrily. "I don't even want to hear about it."

"You didn't testify against me at the trial," he reminded her.

"No," she admitted. "You were my husband, and they couldn't compel me to, but that's the last secret I'm going to keep for you. I hate what you did."

He shifted uncomfortably. "Do you hate me, too?"

He sounded as if he really cared what she felt for him, and her gaze swept over him. He was still a very good-looking man. The years in prison had left only a few marks, and those could have been the natural results of aging. He seemed more subdued, but he'd never been the exuberant type.

"No, Anson, I don't hate you," she assured him, "but I don't love you anymore, either. You killed that with your greed...."

"Dinah, I—"

"No, please, let me finish. It's important that you understand my position. We have no children, so I was able to cut all ties with you when I filed the divorce."

Her voice broke, and she paused to get it under control. "I could have forgiven you if you'd committed a crime in the heat of passion, but to deliberately plan and execute any theft, especially one of that magnitude, reveals a moral depravity that disgusts me."

He looked puzzled rather than repentant. "I don't know why you're so upset. I didn't hurt anybody, the gems were insured." He smiled happily and made an open gesture with his hands. "We're rich, baby. We can leave the country and live anywhere else in the world. We'll never have to worry about money again."

Cold fingers of horror crawled up her spine. For the first time she realized that this man had no conscience. What were people like that called? Sociopaths? How could she have lived with him so long and not suspected?

It would do no good to argue. All she could do was make him understand that she wanted him out of her life.

"*We* won't be doing anything," she said firmly. "I want no part of you or your money. I hadn't expected you to look me up when you got out on parole, and I'm sorry you made the trip because I've put the past behind me and I'm not going back. I like Phoenix. I have a good job, enough money to live on, loyal friends..."

"And a new man?"

Dinah caught her breath. "That's none of your business," she retorted.

He looked sad. "I'll take that to mean yes," he said, but when she opened her mouth to object, he held up his hand. "That wasn't a crack. You're a beautiful and passionate woman. I hadn't expected you to live like a nun."

She almost laughed at the irony of it. If he only knew that's exactly how she'd been living, but not because of any misplaced loyalty to him.

"I just hoped you hadn't remarried," he finished.

She shook her head, stunned by his last remark. "I haven't, but not because I was waiting for you. I like being single."

She paused, debating whether or not to ask the question uppermost in her mind, and finally decided it was important that she know.

"Anson, I'm really mystified." He looked at her and blinked. "I mean, I made it clear how I felt about what you'd done," she continued. "I divorced you as soon as the trial was over, and I haven't been to see you or written to you in prison in all this time. I didn't even tell you where I was, so what made you think I'd come running back to you once you were out?"

He looked away from her. "You were my wife for a long time, Dinah. I love you."

Guilt and exasperation muddled her mind. Had he always been this out of touch with reality, or had it happened gradually over the years he was incarcerated?

She didn't know how to handle the situation, but it had to be done gently. In spite of herself she was moved by the unguarded way he expressed his love for her, leaving himself wide open for any pain she might want to inflict.

"I'm flattered that you still feel that way," she said, her voice husky with pity and regret. "I don't want to hurt you, but you must understand that I can't return your love. You'll be meeting other women now, and I hope you'll discover that your feelings for me are just a habit you've been clinging to. I really do wish you well."

He nodded. "I know you do, and maybe you're right. My contact with women has been pretty restricted for the past five years." He smiled at his understatement, then changed the subject. "I'll have that drink now if the offer's still good."

Dinah fixed drinks, and for the next couple of hours they talked about their lives since they'd last seen each other. Dinah gradually relaxed and actually enjoyed visiting with him. As they chatted, she became aware of how difficult it had been for him to adjust to being locked up, and she struggled with feelings of guilt because she hadn't at least written to him once in a while to relieve some of his boredom.

They were now discussing the conditions of his release. "I have a parole officer, a place to live and a job in Santa Monica that I'm due to start this coming Monday," he told her.

"That's great," she said. "Is it in a jewelry store?"

He shook his head. "Oh, no. I'll never be able to work with precious gems again."

She cringed. Of course he wouldn't. How could she have asked such a thoughtless question?

He must have seen her embarrassment because he smiled at her. "It's all right, I have another marketable skill. Do you remember how I used to like woodworking?"

"How could I forget?" she said. "You built those beautiful new cabinets for our kitchen, and the inlaid coffee table you made me one year for Christmas was the envy of all our friends."

"Yeah, well, my new job is with a firm that makes custom cabinets. I know I'll enjoy it."

"I hope so." Her tone rang with sincerity. "Uh... Anson, have you seen Bernie Rose lately?"

He nodded. "Yeah, I called him when I got out of prison. He'd just returned from a trip to Detroit. Said he'd stopped here to see you." He paused. "It really shook me up when Sarah died. She was so young...."

Dinah sighed. "Yes, she was. Did Bernie tell you that he gave me Sarah's Fabergé egg?"

"He mentioned it. Said Sarah didn't have any family to pass it on to." Anson looked around the room. "What did you do with it? I don't see it anywhere."

"No, I have it put away. Nobody around here knows I have it. I don't think it's wise to display anything so valuable," she explained. "As manager of this apartment complex, I have tenants coming and going in here a lot, and most of them are people I don't know well. I've buried it under my sweaters in the bottom dresser drawer in the bedroom until I find time to go to the bank and rent a safe-deposit—"

The chime of the doorbell cut her sentence off, and she made a face. "Speak of the devil," she muttered as she stood. "Excuse me, that's probably someone with a problem now."

She crossed the room and opened the door to find Todd looking at her from the other side of the screen.

"I hate to bother you," he said, "but my bandage was slipping, and I took it off before I remembered that I didn't have anything to replace it with. Would you by any chance have some gauze and tape?"

In her shock at seeing Anson earlier she'd forgotten to lock the screen, and Todd opened it and walked in while he was talking. His gaze zeroed immediately on Anson. "Oh, I'm sorry, I didn't know you had company."

Anson stood, and Todd walked over to him. "Hi, I'm Todd Campbell," he said, and put out his hand.

Anson took it. "Anson Erhardt," he replied, and looked at the swollen, discolored gash at the base of Todd's head that was partially visible from the front. "What happened to you?"

Todd fingered the lump. "We had a disturbance at the pool yesterday, and I tripped and hit my head. I'm the lifeguard," he mentioned by way of identification, then looked from Anson to Dinah, obviously waiting for one of them to tell him who the stranger was.

Dinah felt a tingle of irritation. There were times when Todd could be a pest, and this was one of them. His timing was such that it almost seemed as if he'd deliberately found an excuse to intrude.

On the other hand that was a nasty-looking bump, and she could tell from his expression that he was hurting. Her resentment melted, and so did her reticence. If she was going to have an intimate relationship with him, and they aroused each other too urgently to resist it much longer, he'd have to be told about Anson.

"Anson is my ex-husband," she said, and was surprised to see a flash of relief in his expression before it changed.

"Oh. I guess I charged in at a bad time." He turned and started for the door.

"No, Todd, wait," she called. "I'll bandage your head. My guest was just getting ready to leave." She looked at the man who had been her husband. "Weren't you, Anson?"

He looked disappointed, but shrugged in resignation. "I guess I was," he said. "May I use your bathroom first?"

"Sure." She pointed across the room. "Through that door and across the hall."

He walked away, and Dinah motioned Todd to follow her into the dining room. "All right," she said, her voice lowered so only he could hear. "Now tell me what it is you really want."

He looked startled. "I told you—"

"So now tell me the truth. You know better than anyone that we have a large, well-stocked first-aid kit locked in a cupboard in the recreation hall. You've used it several times when children have scraped themselves while playing in the wading pool."

He grinned and actually looked embarrassed. "Oh, yeah, I guess I forgot."

She grinned back. "I guess you did." She raised her hand and gently caressed the lacerated area. "Does it still hurt?"

He put his arms around her and drew her close. "Yes," he whispered, "but what hurt even more was knowing there was a man in here with you all afternoon. I've been going crazy."

She tensed and removed her hand. "Have you been spying on me?"

He shrugged. "Not spying, just observing. I saw him when he drove up, and every time I looked out of the window after that, he was still here. I'm sorry I blundered in the way I did, but I was worried. You hadn't told me you were expecting a visit from your ex-husband."

The last sentence had an accusing ring, and Dinah realized that he was jealous. Well, why not? She certainly wouldn't have wanted him spending an afternoon behind closed doors with another woman, certainly not an ex-wife.

She put her hand back up and tangle her fingers in his blond curls. "I wasn't," she assured him. "I'll tell you about it later. Now, let me go, I don't want him to know that we're . . . um . . . involved."

For a moment his arms tightened around her, and she was afraid he was going to get possessive, but then he abruptly released her and stepped back.

"I'll make myself scarce and come back after he leaves," he said, and headed for the door.

When Anson appeared a few minutes later, he looked around. "Where's the blond hunk?"

Dinah was still standing in the dining area where Todd had left her. "He went to get a first-aid kit," she told him. "He'll be back in a minute."

They stood facing each other as an awkward silence developed between them.

It was Anson who finally broke it. "Are you sure there's no chance that you'll come back to me, Dinah?" He looked and sounded so woebegone that she could almost feel sorry for him.

"I'm sure. We're both different people than we were when we first got married. I . . . I wish you'd give the diamonds back."

It was the first time either of them had mentioned the gems directly during their afternoon together.

He looked startled. "No way! I paid for them with five years of my life. Those diamonds are mine."

He turned and left as abruptly as he'd come.

Chapter Nine

As Todd walked across the driveway, he flashed a prearranged hand signal to the man sitting a block and a half away in a nondescript gray car. The man flashed one back, and Todd knew the backup operative he'd hurriedly arranged for earlier was alerted and ready to follow Anson Erhardt to the ends of the earth if necessary.

It was only a few minutes later as Todd watched from his window that Erhardt came out of Dinah's apartment and got into his Camaro. The sports car would be an easy mark to follow, and Todd stood behind the white curtains while Erhardt made a U-turn in the middle of the driveway and headed back toward the public thoroughfare, the gray car in pursuit.

Todd dropped down into the desk chair and rubbed his pounding head with the heel of his hand. He could relax now that Dinah's ex-husband was finally gone. The operative, Hal Quincy, was not only good at tracking but also reliable.

Todd had alerted Wesley Nelson in L.A. as soon as Erhardt had arrived at Dinah's apartment, and Wes had assured him that they wouldn't drop the ball at that end again. After that, the time had dragged agonizingly by with no indication of what was taking place inside the apartment between Dinah and the man who was once her husband.

Who may also be her partner in crime.

Todd cringed, and the pressure in his head increased. Damn! Why did Erhardt have to show up today of all days? Up to the time of the accident he'd felt fine, and tomorrow he'd probably be functioning okay again, but today the tension escalated the pain in his head until he couldn't even think, let alone make intelligent decisions about the woman who was more important to him than anything else.

Probably even more than his own honor.

At least she'd told him the truth this time. What a relief it had been when she admitted that the man with her was her ex-husband. He'd hated having to force a confrontation, because he wasn't sure what he'd have done if she'd lied and said Erhardt was a friend or prospective tenant.

With a soft groan he straightened up and reached for the bottle of pills on the desk. He'd only taken one in the early afternoon because two, the prescribed amount, made him drowsy, but now the pain was more disabling than the drowsiness.

He shook two tablets into his hand, swallowed them, then folded his arms on the desk in front of him and laid his head on them. As soon as the ache subsided a little, he'd go over and hold Dinah to her promise to tell him about her afternoon with Erhardt.

Maybe she'd also put her arms around him and hold him, let him relax in her soft embrace and massage the kinks out of the screaming muscles in his shoulders. He closed his eyes and sighed.

Oh, Dinah, don't abuse my trust. I love you so much.

Dinah took the last batch of chocolate-chip cookies from the oven and glanced at her watch for the umpteenth time.

Where on earth was Todd? He'd said he'd come back as soon as Anson left, but that was an hour ago, and she hadn't seen or heard from him since.

She slid the hot cookies from the pan to the rack where the others were cooling and set the pan down on the stove.

It wasn't like him not to come when he said he would. Was he all right? He hadn't looked well. His pallor had been gray underneath the tan, and there were lines at his mouth and a pounding pulse in his forehead that could have indicated pain, or a queasy stomach, or both. He'd admitted that his head hurt.

With jerky movements she tossed her apron across the breakfast bar as she headed for the door. She knew she was behaving like a mother hen, or an impatient lover, but she had to know if there was something wrong.

In the recreation room she was delayed for several minutes by people wanting to know how Todd was and when the pool would open again. When she finally managed to excuse herself, she hurried to his door and knocked.

There was no answer.

She knocked again and waited.

Still no answer.

Had he gone out somewhere? That didn't seem likely because she'd been standing at the kitchen window while she made cookies, and the window fronted on the driveway. She probably would have seen him.

Maybe he was asleep. That seemed more likely. He'd been badly battered yesterday, even unconscious for a while, and then with the strong medication he was taking...

She turned the knob, and the door came unlatched. It wasn't locked!

She continued to rest her hand on the knob. Should she go in? She hated invading his privacy, but what if he was sick or even unconscious?

Opening the door a crack, she called his name. There was no answer. Alarmed, she swung it wide and went in.

Todd was sitting at the desk beneath the window with his arms folded in front of him and his head resting on them.

She walked over and put her hand on his shoulder. He was asleep. Gently she shook him. "Todd, are you all right? Wake up."

He flexed his shoulders but slept on.

She shook him again, harder this time. "Todd. Wake up and move over to the bed. You can't be comfortable in that position."

He shifted and mumbled something, then settled down to sleep again.

Her gaze wandered to the pill container sitting on the desk. Was it possible that he'd lost track and taken more medication than he should have?

She picked up the bottle and poured the contents into her hand. The prescription had been for fifteen and there were still eight left, which meant that he'd taken one less than allowed.

This time she shook him harder and raised her voice. "Todd, it's Dinah. Wake up and let me help you get into bed where you can be more comfortable."

To her relief he raised his head and looked around, obviously dazed and confused. "What? Dinah?" He turned his head and saw her, and his dulled eyes widened. "Dinah! What are you doing here?" Sitting up, he looked at his watch. "Oh, no! Have I been asleep?"

He rubbed his hands over his face as if to wipe away his stupor.

"You certainly have," she told him, and put her hand to his temple. It was warm and moist but probably from sleep rather than fever. "When you didn't come back after Anson left, I came looking for you. Your door was unlocked, and I had a hard time rousing you."

He turned in the chair and put his arms around her waist, then cradled his head in the valley between her breasts. "Dinah, love, you've got your verbs all wrong," he said with a contented sigh. "You may have had trouble waking me, but you arouse me just by walking into the room. Now what was it you were saying about us going to bed?"

She put her arms around him and leaned down to rub her cheek in his hair. "I said I'm going to help you lie down. Otherwise you'll wind up back in the hospital."

He kissed the rise of her breast. "I feel better since that nap, but if you're so anxious to get me in bed, I'll be happy to oblige."

He nuzzled the place he'd just kissed and sent tremors along her spine. "Now hold on there, buster," she teased. "It's you who's going to bed, not me."

"Tell you what," he said as one hand settled on her derriere. "I'll lie down if you'll join me."

She knew she'd do whatever he wanted, but it seemed prudent to at least make a stab at establishing a few ground rules. "If I do, will you behave yourself?"

His hand moved caressingly over her bottom. "Do I have to?" he asked impishly.

She chuckled and reached back to move his hand up to her waist. "Yes, you have to," she assured him.

He moved it back down and swatted her playfully. "Oh, well, what the hell," he groused. "I'll take you any way I can get you."

He stood, then swayed and grabbed the back of the chair as Dinah reached out in alarm. "Todd, what's the matter?" She put her arm around his waist to steady him. "First I couldn't wake you up, and now you can't stand alone. I really do think I should take you back to the hospital."

"No," he said as he righted himself. "I'm okay. Really. It's those pills I've been taking. They make me drowsy and light-headed. I think they're too strong."

He put his arm across her shoulders, and together they walked to the bed. She pulled back the blanket and top sheet, then told him to lie down. He did, and she sat on the edge and began untying his shoes.

"Hey, you don't have to do that," he protested. "I can take off my own shoes."

She looked at him and smiled. "I know you can, but I'd like to do it for you."

He grinned and raised his knees to make his feet more accessible. "In that case, sweetheart, I'm all yours. Feel free to remove anything you like. Just remember that if the jeans go, all promises of behaving myself go with them."

She felt the silly blush that she should have outgrown long ago. "The shoes will be quite enough," she said, and hurriedly removed them.

He moved over and patted the space he'd vacated. "Come here and let me hold you." His voice vibrated with warmth.

Her embarrassment as well as any doubts she may have had melted, and she stepped out of her low-heeled pumps and crawled into his arms.

Todd cuddled her against him and sought her mouth. She gave it eagerly, and their lips and tongues embraced and vibrated to the rhythm of their ardor. Her palms roamed over his back as one of his cupped her breast while the other continued its fascination with her firm buttocks.

When he used that hand to pull up her skirt and caress her nylon-covered thigh, she knew it was time to call a halt. It cost her dearly, but she managed to break off the kiss and bury her face in his shoulder. "We...we'd better cool it a little," she stammered, and could feel his heart beating as fast as her own.

"If that's what you want," he said gently, although Dinah could hear the underlying frustration he couldn't entirely mask. His hold on her loosened just enough to put a little distance between them.

In an apparent effort to deflect the building urgency, he asked, "Are you still willing to tell what your ex-husband was doing here?"

He sounded relaxed, but she could feel the tension in him. Much as she hated discussing her aborted marriage, she knew that for Todd's peace of mind it had to be done.

"Anson has been in prison in southern California for the past five years and was just released on parole a few days ago."

She held her breath, unsure of what Todd's reaction might be, although she expected him to be shocked. Instead his tenseness eased somewhat, and instead of asking the obvious question—What did he do?—he said, "And the first thing he did when he got out was come to you."

She nodded, too surprised to say anything but, "Yes."

"Does he want you to go back to him?" His tone was clipped, almost impersonal.

Again she nodded. "Yes."

She felt his muscles clench even tighter than before. "Are you going to?"

That snapped her out of her confusion, and she pulled away from him. "How can you ask such a question?" she demanded, and sat up.

He sat up, too, and grasped her arms so she couldn't escape. "Please, Dinah, I have to know." The coldness of his tone had been replaced with anguish. "Are you still in love with him?"

She began to understand. He was afraid she might still be attracted to the man she'd married and divorced.

Her voice softened. "No, I'm not. If I were, do you honestly think I'd be here in bed with you?"

He blinked, and a sheepish expression replaced the anguished one. "No, I guess you wouldn't," he admitted. "It's just that I haven't had much experience with jealousy, and it's eating me alive."

He put his arms around her and lay back down, taking her with him. She landed partway across his chest, and her gaze held his as she lowered her face to kiss him tenderly. "Is it, really?" she murmured, and couldn't hold back a small smile. "Now you know how I felt the day I came home from Tucson and found you frolicking with our very own Miss Junior Stripper."

He raised one eyebrow. "Frolicking?" The word came out as a teasing yelp. "I'll have you know I was not frolicking with Lynette. I was merely sitting at the table with her, contemplating reasonably lawful ways to get rid of her."

He tangled his hand in her long hair that tumbled onto his chest. "Besides," he continued more seriously, "you didn't act jealous. You were as cool, calm and poised as ever.''

She nipped him lovingly on the chin. "That's only because I knew that if I followed my instinct and threw the little baggage in the pool, I'd probably get both sued and fired. Performing acts of mayhem on the tenants is a breach of etiquette for a property manager.''

He raised his hand to caress the back of her neck under her hair. "Dinah, my darling," he said huskily "you can perform acts on me any time you want to, and I promise not to sue you.''

She knew he wasn't talking mayhem. "Oh? What kind of acts did you have in mind?'' The pictures her imagination was projecting made her heart skip beats.

"Any kind you want," he replied. "And if you run out of ideas, I'd be happy to supply some.''

He pushed gently on the back of her head to bring it down so he could kiss her without having to raise his. Their lips clung, and for a long time they lay like that, savoring the intimacy, and the pleasure, of making love without the clawing urgency of passion.

This was something she'd never known with Anson, never even thought was possible until Todd had introduced her to it. She'd experienced Todd's passion, and knew that, unleashed, it was explosive and, therefore, difficult to rein in. She suspected that few men were willing to make the effort to hold their lust in check, or, more importantly, to make themselves that vulnerable to the woman in their lives.

This time Todd broke off the kiss. "I think we're getting off the subject," he said unsteadily. "I hate to go from the sublime to the mundane, but we were talking about Anson Erhardt. What did he do that got him sent to prison?''

Dinah laid her cheek against Todd's chest and sighed. "He was convicted of stealing diamonds from his employer."

Todd massaged her back. "How did he do that?"

"He says he didn't. He pleaded not guilty."

"But he was convicted anyway?"

"Yes." She shifted uncomfortably, and raised her head. "Look, Todd, I really don't—"

"I know, love." He cradled her head against his chest once more. "This is painful for you, and I'm sorry, but bear with me a little longer. It's not just idle curiosity, I really do need to know about this important part of your past."

She could understand; she'd want to know about his divorce if he'd ever had one. If only she didn't feel so disloyal when discussing Anson's crime with others. There really wasn't any need for her to; he'd given up his right to privacy when he stole another person's property.

"All right," she said reluctantly. "There were several theories about how he made off with the gems, but all the prosecutors were able to prove was that they were gone and Anson took them."

"Did he?" Todd asked, so softly that she had to strain to hear.

Her stomach muscles clenched. She hated evasion. "The jury said he did."

"Do you believe them?"

Dinah hated lying even more. "I didn't at first," she said hesitantly, "but by the end of the trial I did. That's why I divorced him. I'd never have left if I'd believed him innocent."

She soothed her conscience by acknowledging that none of what she'd said was a lie. She just didn't tell him that it wasn't the jury who changed her mind but Anson, himself, when he confessed his guilt to her. She could never betray him by revealing that. He'd been her husband at the time, and now he'd paid the legal price for his crime. As far as she was concerned, the subject was closed. Finished.

Apparently Todd didn't think so. "Do you ever regret the divorce?"

Again she pulled away from him and sat up. "Of course I regret the divorce," she snapped. "It was a brutally painful time for me, and I bitterly resented that the husband I'd loved, who claimed to love me, had done something so counter to everything I believed in that I could no longer stay married to him."

She turned and looked down at Todd. "I hope you never have to go through a divorce, Todd, but if you do, you'll know why I don't want to talk about mine. I sometimes think the death of love is even more painful than the death of a loved one."

She swung her legs off the bed and put her feet in her pumps. "At least when a loved one dies it's a clean break, final." There was sorrow in her tone. "When love dies, it's a wrenching, guilt-ridden thing that never seems to end."

Before Todd could stop her, she stood and strode out of the room.

She almost made it to her front door before he caught up with her. Catching her from behind by the shoulders he pulled her back against him. "Don't run away from me, sweetheart," he said breathlessly, and nuzzled her ear. "I'm sorry. I didn't mean to dredge up painful memories, but maybe this is something you need to talk about. I suspect you've had it bottled up for too long."

She leaned into his embrace. "I didn't know you were a psychologist," she muttered.

"There are a lot of things you don't know about me." He nibbled at her lobe. "But we'll discuss that later. Now, come on, let's go inside before we shock the neighbors."

In the living room, Dinah sat down in a chair and motioned Todd to the sofa. She wanted to remain out of touching distance from him until this conversation was over. For a moment he looked as if he was going to protest the separation, but then he apparently thought better of it and dropped down on the couch.

"There are only a couple of other things I need to know, honey," he said. "Do you mind?"

She settled into the comfortable chair. "I won't know until you tell me what they are."

He smiled. "Right. Were the diamonds returned to their owner?"

She shook her head. "No, they were never recovered. Anson said he was innocent and knew nothing of the stones."

She could read his next question as plainly as if it were written across his forehead, and held up her hand. "Don't bother to ask," she said. "No, I don't know where they are, either. If Anson did indeed take them, I have no idea what he did with them, and frankly I don't want to know. It has nothing to do with me."

She looked at her watch. "It's dinnertime. If you'd like to stay, I have a tuna casserole in the freezer, but I'm warning you, I've said all I'm going to about Anson. You can be thinking of another subject while I put the casserole in the oven."

When Todd got back to his room at a little after nine, the red light was blinking on his answering machine. It was Wes with the message to call him.

"Wes, this is Todd," he said when the other man answered his ring. "What's happening with Erhardt?"

"That's what I called about," Wes said. "Your man, Quincy, followed him to the airport where he turned in his rental car and booked passage to LAX on the first flight out, which is nonstop and due to land at ten o'clock. Quincy called me, and we've got a couple of men there now waiting to pick up Erhardt's trail when he gets in."

Todd breathed a sigh of relief. "Great. I spent the afternoon with Dinah and finally got her to talk about her ex-husband and the divorce. Everything she said was right on the button as we know it. She didn't lie about anything, although I suspect she held a few things back."

"Don't they always?" Wes observed wryly. "That's one of the perils of trying to get people to tell what they don't want to."

"Yeah," Todd agreed. "She swears she doesn't know where the diamonds are, and I believe her."

"Why?" The question was crisp and curt.

"Why? Well, just because I do—"

"That's no reason. You know she's lied to you in the past. Why do you believe her now?"

Todd's temper began to simmer. "If you'll stop interrupting, I'll tell you. She hasn't so much lied to me before as evaded the truth, but this time she agreed to talk about it and even answered some pretty probing questions about her feelings on the matter."

"Sure, but that doesn't let her off the hook. How do you know she answered them truthfully? Come on, Campbell, what's the matter with you? You've been conned before. Are you sure that blow on the head didn't dull your reflexes?"

Todd resented his attitude. "Damn it, Wes, there's nothing wrong with my reflexes or anything else. I'm

rained to read body language and voice inflections, and I
ust don't think she has the stones."

"Probably not," Wes agreed, "but that doesn't mean
she doesn't know where they are. Keep a close eye on her.
Use that head injury as an excuse not to go back to work
at the pool for the next few days and stick close to her.

"Meanwhile, we're sure as hell not going to lose Erhardt again. He's spent five years in the slammer for those
diamonds, you can bet he's going to retrieve them now. We
intend to be there when he does."

On Wednesday, Todd felt better, but he kept the appointment Dinah had made for him with a physician for a
follow-up examination. The doctor agreed that he was recovering well, but advised him not to go back to work for
the rest of the week.

Todd was grateful for the legitimate opportunity to
monitor Dinah's activity, but he loathed spying on her.

Would this monstrous deception ever end? He was the
one who was betraying her trust, and each time he did, it
sickened him. When this was finally over, would there be
even a remote chance that he'd be able to justify it to her?

Meanwhile, according to Wes Nelson, Erhardt had arrived as expected back in Los Angeles and was living in an
apartment in Santa Monica, not far from where he was
scheduled to start work on Monday.

It was midmorning on Thursday that a police car drove
up in front of Dinah's apartment and an officer got out
and walked to the door. Todd was sitting in his usual place
in front of the window, watching a talk show on television
to relieve the boredom, and he sprang to attention to watch
as Dinah let the man in.

Good Lord, what had happened?

Todd lost no time tearing across the driveway. Dinah's door was open, the screen unlocked, and he stalked in without bothering to knock as she and the policeman, who were standing in the living room, looked up, startled.

"Dinah, what's going on?" he demanded as he walked over to her.

"Oh, Todd," she said, making an effort to keep her voice steady. "I've been robbed!"

He gasped, and looked around. As far as he could tell, nothing had been disturbed. "But how? When?"

"I don't know. I just discovered that it was gone."

"Just what is it that's missing, ma'am?" asked the officer.

"My egg," Dinah wailed.

Todd knew what she was talking about, but the officer stared at her in disgust, obviously writing her off as a fruitcake.

"What kind of egg, honey?" Todd asked quickly, since he couldn't explain for her without letting her know he'd searched her place.

"It's a Fabergé egg. A valuable work of art that was the family heirloom of a friend of mine who's dead now." She looked at Todd. "It belonged to Bernie Rose's wife. He brought it to me when he was here the other day. Sarah had no children, and he said she'd wa-want me to have it."

A sob shook her, and he reached out and took her in his arms. Thank God, she'd reported the theft to the police and was being open and honest about it, which was a pretty clear sign that the object had nothing to do with the diamond heist. He should have known better than to doubt her.

"Don't cry," he said soothingly. "The police will find it."

"But . . . but what if they don't? I promised Bernie I'd take good care of it, and now it's gone."

Another sob escaped, but this time she pulled away from Todd and wiped at her tears with a tissue she held in her hand. "I never should have kept it here. I should have taken it to the bank the very next day and rented a safe-deposit box to put it in, but I've been busy and—"

Her voice caught, and once more she dabbed at her eyes.

"Was it insured?" the officer asked.

Dinah looked thoughtful. "I don't know. Bernie didn't say anything about it, and I didn't think to ask. I know it wouldn't be covered for the full amount by my renter's policy, but money isn't the point . . ."

"Where in the house did you keep it?" he interrupted. "Was it in plain sight or hidden away?"

"It was wrapped in tissue paper and packed inside a white gift box in my bottom dresser drawer in the bedroom. I put it there, under my sweaters, right after Bernie left that night. I intended to take it to the bank for safe-keeping, but I was busy and the days slid by and . . ."

The policeman was writing in a notebook. "When was the last time you saw it?"

"I took it out a couple of days later just to hold it and look at it. It brought back memories of happier times when . . . when my friend was alive. Then I packed it in the box and put it back under my sweaters, and I haven't seen it since."

"How did you discover it was missing?"

She sank down on the arm of the sofa. "I had some business at the bank this morning so I was going to take the egg with me and get that taken care of, too. When I opened the bottom drawer I noticed that my sweaters were all jumbled up instead of in neat piles the way I'd put them. I grabbed the box and opened it, but the egg was gone."

The policeman scribbled notes for a minute, then looked at Todd. "Mind telling me who you are?"

Todd swiftly slipped into his college-kid act. "Todd Campbell," he said breezily, and put out his hand. "I'm the lifeguard here. I have a room in the rec building right across the driveway." He motioned to the front of the house.

The officer shook his hand. "Officer Irwin," he replied, and glanced at the discolored gash at the base of Todd's skull. "What happened to you?"

Both Todd and Dinah explained about the accident at the pool. "Since the doc says I can't go back to work until Monday, I was sitting in front of my window, watching television, when I saw you drive up," Todd said in conclusion. "Naturally I was concerned about Dinah so I came over."

The officer turned his attention to Dinah. "How many people knew you had this valuable art object?"

She shrugged. "Nobody. I'm resident manager for this apartment complex so there are people coming and going here all day. That's why I hid it in the drawer instead of putting it on display. I didn't tell anybody I had it."

Officer Irwin gestured toward Todd. "How about your neighbor, here? Didn't you tell him?"

Dinah shook her head. "No. There was no reason to. He didn't know any of the people involved with it. It would have taken a lot of explaining, and since I was going to put it in a safe-deposit box where no one would see it, there wasn't any reason to mention it."

The policeman closed his notebook. "I'd like to examine the bedroom now, and I'll need a description of the article. Since you last saw it, have you had any suspicion that someone may have broken in or gone through your things?"

"No, I haven't," she said, "but I have a good idea of when it happened."

Both Todd and Irwin looked at her as she continued. "When Todd was injured at the pool on Monday, I ran out of the house without thinking about anything but getting over there. Then I rode with him in the ambulance to the hospital and stayed until he was released. I was away from the apartment for four and a half or five hours, and when I got back, I discovered the door wide open."

She shook her head in disbelief. "I was so upset that I'd not only forgotten to lock it, I'd even forgotten to shut it."

"Did it occur to you to look around and see if anything was out of place or missing?"

"Of course," Dinah said. "I looked through all the rooms, but nothing had been touched. I remember thinking how lucky I was."

"Did you check to see if the egg was still in its box in the drawer?"

She sighed. "No. To tell you the truth, I forgot all about it."

The policeman looked skeptical.

"I'd only had it a few days, and there was nothing out of place," she said defensively. "I know it was stupid but, well, I just wasn't thinking straight, and there was no sign of anyone having been in the apartment."

"Yes, ma'am," he said. "Are you sure there's nothing else missing today?"

"I'm very sure," she answered crisply. "I have a few pieces of fine jewelry in a top drawer of the same chest, but they're still right where I left them."

"All right, then, if you'll show me to the bedroom...." He turned and looked at Todd. "Oh, we won't need you anymore now, Mr. Campbell, but I'll probably want to talk to you later."

It was a dismissal if Todd ever heard one, but he wasn't going to be bullied. His gaze sought Dinah's. "Do you want me to stay?"

She gave him an appreciative smile but shook her head. "No, there's no need. I'll talk to you later."

He didn't argue because he had some serious thinking to do. There was something not right about that damned egg, but it kept eluding him.

This wasn't a random burglary. Whoever had done it had come into the house, gone straight to the bedroom and taken it out of the drawer.

If she was telling the truth, and he was sure she was, then how did the burglar know she had it and where it was hidden? And while he was about it, why didn't he take the jewelry? Those rings and jeweled combs were worth several thousand dollars, and they were in the same chest.

There were a lot of loose ends in this case, and somewhere was a link that would hook them all together. It was time for him to come out from under cover and take the long chance that Dinah cared enough about him to understand and forgive his trespassing against her.

He couldn't put it off any longer. He had to find that link, and a gut instinct told him the place to start was with Orville Fischbeck, the art appraiser.

Chapter Ten

Orville Fischbeck listened intently as Todd, who this time admitted to being a private investigator, sat across the desk from him and told him about the strange disappearance of the Fabergé egg the appraiser had recently examined.

"I guess what I need to know," Todd said in conclusion, "is what there is about it that would make somebody take the risk of stealing it but pass up other valuables that could be taken just as easily?"

Fischbeck shook his head. "That's what's so puzzling. The egg you brought in the other day has a certain amount of extra value to a collector because it was made in the Fabergé workshop, but it was just a shell. A beautiful shell, but there were no jewels and no surprise. On the underground market it would take time to sell and wouldn't bring as much as the jewelry you described would."

Surprise. The word jarred Todd. Fischbeck had used it the last time they'd talked, but something else had come

up, and Todd had let it pass without asking for an expla
nation.

"Back up a minute," he said. "What is this 'surprise'
you keep talking about?"

The appraiser raised one eyebrow. "Oh, didn't I tell
you? The Fabergé eggs made for the czars could be
opened, revealing the 'surprise,' as it was called. Inside
there might be a basket of flowers made of precious
metals, or the top of the egg might fly open every hour to
reveal a jeweled rooster that crowed and flapped its wings.
Why, one of them even had—"

Fischbeck's explanation touched a nerve that made
Todd reel. "Are you telling me that those eggs are hollow
and can be opened?" he bellowed.

My God, if that were true...

"Most of them, yes," replied the startled appraiser,
"but not the one you brought in here. I examined it care
fully since some of the springs were cleverly hidden in
those eggs, but this one had none."

"But it was hollow?"

"Yes, of course."

Todd felt like hitting his forehead with the heel of his
hand. Damn. Damn. Damn. How could he have missed
the obvious?

The diamonds were in the egg!

Todd could only speculate how they'd been placed there,
but it was plain that Erhardt had taken it with him when
he left Dinah's apartment, and it was Bernard Rose who
was his accomplice, not Dinah!

In his shock and excitement he barely remembered tell
ing the little man goodbye and rushing out of the office.

Dinah sat on the sofa with her hands clutched in her lap
and stared into space. She'd been like that ever since the

policeman had finished his investigation and left. Her mind had simply shut down. No matter how hard she tried to think, it refused to function.

There had to be more to this theft than appeared on the surface, but when she tried to probe her memory, she came up with a blank. Between the numbing shock and the overwhelming guilt, it was no wonder she couldn't reason.

The guilt was the worst. She'd have to tell Bernie, but how could she? He'd trusted her to cherish Sarah's heirloom and keep it safe. Instead, she'd tossed it in a drawer, and then left the apartment wide open for hours with no thought of—

The loud ring of the doorbell interrupted her musing, and she jumped. Now what?

She got up and went to the door to find Officer Irwin back again. This time Todd was with him. A sober, unsmiling Todd.

"Sorry to bother you again, Ms. Swensen," the officer said, "but something has come up that we need to discuss with you."

We? Why was he including Todd? And why was Todd with him now when he'd plainly been dismissed a couple of hours earlier?

"All right," she said as she unlocked the screen and pushed it open. "Come in."

Maybe she was mistaken. It was possible that the two men had just happened to arrive at her door at the same time.

"Todd," she said. "Did you want something?"

He looked at her, but before he could answer, the officer spoke. "He's with me."

More puzzled than ever, she gestured toward the living room. "Oh, well, if this is going to take a while, we'd better sit down and be comfortable."

She gestured Officer Irwin to a chair, and she and Todd sat on the sofa. So far Todd hadn't said a word, which was totally unlike him. He was strictly the verbose type, whether carefree or angry, happy or sad, he always had something to say about it.

Her foreboding increased.

It was Irwin who dropped the bombshell. "It's come to my attention that you were visited on Tuesday by your ex-husband." He glanced at his ever present notebook then continued "Anson Erhardt, who has recently been paroled from prison—"

"How do you know that?" Dinah interrupted. "Nobody here knows about Anson...."

The truth hit her with a crippling blow, and she turned to Todd. "It was you." Disbelief warred with certainty in her tone. "I thought I could trust you. I only told you about my messy divorce because I thought you..."

Her voice broke, and she choked back the words *loved me,* and clamped her mouth shut.

Todd winced and wiped his hand over his face. "Dinah, I...I'm sorry..."

"Sorry doesn't cut it," she said, too angry to care that they had an audience. "You knew how painful that part of my past is for me. Just for once, couldn't you have kept your mouth shut and not blabbed everything you know?"

She saw his anguished expression, but this time he'd gone too far. She wasn't going to forgive him easily.

He reached out to her, but when she backed away, he dropped his arms. "Oh, sweetheart, it's keeping my mouth shut that's landed me in this impossible situation," he said, and she deliberately ignored the pain in his tone. "My sins are legion, and I deeply regret every one of them."

He turned to the policeman. "Could you give us a few minutes alone together? This won't take long, I promise."

Irwin nodded and stood. "I'll wait in the car," he said, and left.

Dinah was still too angry to catch the significance of what Todd was saying. She watched the officer leave, still fuming but waiting until they were alone to light into him again.

When the door closed, she was trying to sort out in her mind what she wanted to say, but Todd spoke first. His tone was clear and concise, with only a hint of the emotion so evident before.

"There's no way I can soften this, Dinah, so I'll just give it to you straight. I didn't come to Phoenix from Florida to go to law school. I came from Los Angeles for the sole purpose of trying to find out if you either had the diamonds your ex-husband stole, or if you knew where they were."

He reached in his back pocket and brought out his billfold as Dinah blinked uncomprehendingly. Obviously her mind was still not functioning right. He hadn't even known about Anson and the theft then.

He withdrew a business card from his wallet and handed it to her. "I'm a private investigator with a firm in Los Angeles that has been hired by the insurance company to try to find the gems Anson Erhardt stole. We knew he was coming up for parole soon, and figured that he'd retrieve the diamonds as soon as he was out of prison."

She took the card in her shaking hand but didn't attempt to read it. "You're a detective?" she asked inanely.

"Not quite. At least not a police detective. I'm what's called an operative. You know, like Spenser, or Mike

Hammer, only I work for a large firm instead of on my own.''

"And you think I have the diamonds?" She wished it wasn't so hard for her to concentrate. If only the fog in her brain would go away.

"No! That is, not anymore. In the beginning it seemed likely, but once I met you, got to know you, I never really believed you were involved."

His tone was heating up, becoming more intense. She wondered absently if he'd been taught that trick. "Then why didn't you go back to Los Angeles?"

He ran his fingers through his tousled hair. "I couldn't. My hunches didn't mean anything to the insurance company. They wanted proof. I had to get it for them."

Her confusion was beginning to lift now, and as conflicting emotions struggled for dominance, she realized she'd made a bad mistake by not being grateful for its protection. "So you stayed here and made love to me so I'd tell you all my secrets." It was a statement of fact, not a question.

Todd came to life then. "Oh, God, no! Dinah, you've got to understand. I fell in love with you. I wasn't seducing you for information, I just couldn't be near you and not hold you, kiss you . . . ''

He continued to talk, but Dinah wasn't listening. How could she have been so blind? Of course a kid like Todd, bright, athletic and ambitious, wouldn't be attracted to an older woman who'd been a wife and a divorcée for longer than he'd been shaving.

Had she really been that desperate for a man? If so, she hadn't been aware of it until he came along with his boyish smile, his muscle builder's body and his kisses that left her weak with longing.

She swallowed back a giggle. Actually, it was pretty funny. He must have laughed about it with his friends. Wasn't there a running joke about older women making fools of themselves over young men?

The giggle was back, and it became a full-fledged laugh before she could choke it down again. It sounded loud in the quiet room, and was quickly followed by another, then another.

"Dinah. Dinah, what are you laughing about?"

She heard Todd calling to her, but she couldn't stop long enough to answer.

"Dinah, stop it!" He was shaking her, gently but firmly. "Honey, don't, please don't get hysterical. I meant every word I said. I know it's hard now, but just try to believe me."

She hadn't heard what he'd been saying before, but the word *hysterical* caught her attention, and she quit laughing as suddenly as she'd started. Dinah Swensen had never been hysterical in her life, not even when her husband was arrested for grand theft, and she wasn't going to let a young stud with more ambition than ethics make her break down now.

She stiffened and pulled away from him. "Ask Officer Irwin to come back in," she said in her frostiest tone. "I'd like to get this over with."

He looked at her, and she was forced to recognize his concern. "Are you sure you're all right? Dinah, did you hear any of what I was saying to you?"

She wasn't going to sit there and argue her sanity. Instead, she rose and went after the policeman herself, with Todd right behind her, protesting.

Back in the living room they sat down again, but this time Dinah sat in the chair and left the couch to Todd and

Irwin. She was aware of the officer's glance, and knew he was trying to gauge her emotional condition.

Damn Todd for putting her in such an embarrassing position!

Cooly she crossed her legs and folded her hands lightly in her lap. When neither of the men spoke immediately, she broke the silence.

"If you don't mind, I'm a working woman and I have a lot of things to take care of, so could we get on with whatever it is you want of me?"

The two men looked at each other, and Todd apparently got the go-ahead. "Dinah, I'm sorry but I have to ask this. Did you tell Anson that you had the egg and where it was hidden?"

Anson? Oh, good heavens, she hadn't even considered that he might have taken it. But why would he?

"He already knew I had it," she said slowly. "Bernie . . . uh, Mr. Rose . . . had mentioned it to him. We discussed it, and he asked what I'd done with it since he didn't see it on display. I told him. There was no reason not to. He steals jewelry, not art objects."

She cringed at her own words. That last sentence was crude and uncalled for. She'd have to be more careful of what she said.

"Did he go into the bedroom at any time after that?" Todd asked.

She thought for a moment. "No. The only time he was out of my sight was when he went to the bathroom just before he left."

"You mean while I was still here?"

"Yes." She was beginning to see what he was getting at.

"Now think carefully," he said. "You and I were in the dining room talking and not paying any attention to what was going on in the rest of the apartment. Isn't it possible that he could have ducked into the bedroom instead of the bathroom, taken the egg out of the box and slipped it into his inside jacket pocket where a slight bulge wouldn't be noticeable?''

She didn't have to think about it. ''Yes, it is possible, but why would he? He must have known I'd notify the police when I discovered it gone, and he's on parole. If he was convicted of another theft, he'd go back to prison for a long time.''

She couldn't miss the look of compassion for her that flitted across Todd's face. ''Honey,'' he said gently. ''We're almost certain that the diamonds were inside the egg.''

It was too much coming at her too fast. She couldn't cope with the implications. It would mean that her dear friend, Bernie, was an accomplice, and that he and her ex-husband had deliberately put her at risk to keep their stolen loot safe.

''No,'' she cried, and clutched at the arms of the chair. ''How could they be? The egg doesn't open. There's no way to get them in there.''

Todd stood and started to go to her, but when she shrank back, he turned and went to the kitchen instead, leaving Irwin to explain. ''Mr. Erhardt is a jeweler, and according to Todd, the egg was encrusted with gold. It would be a simple matter for him to remove some of the gold, saw the egg in two and insert the gems and whatever he used to cushion them so they wouldn't rattle. Then to put it back together and disguise the seam with the gold when he replaced it. Not even the appraiser would catch it.''

Dinah heard more than the policeman realized he was telling. When had Todd seen the egg? She hadn't even told him she had it, and Anson was no longer in Phoenix.

And when had the egg been appraised? She hadn't had it done, and Bernie sure wouldn't have entrusted it to an appraiser if he knew it was filled with two million dollars' worth of diamonds.

She was afraid she knew the answer, but she had to hear it from Todd.

He came back just then, carrying a glass half full of a golden liquid and handed it to her. "Here. It's brandy. Sip it. It'll help, I promise."

She almost started laughing again. His promises came as easily as his lies, and were probably just as worthless.

She set the glass on the lamp table beside her and looked up at him. "Todd, how did you know what the egg looked like? And who had it appraised? I didn't."

With a groan he lowered his head and looked away. "I did," he said. "I searched your apartment while you were in Tucson. When I found the egg, I took it out and had it appraised, then put it back."

The numbness that had encased Dinah melted into a hot, burning rage. Slowly and with great dignity she rose from the chair and picked up the glass beside her.

Turning to face Todd, who was standing just inches away, she tightened her fingers around it and drew her arm back slightly.

"You bastard!" she said, and managed to put all her contempt and despair into the two words as she tossed the brandy full force into his face.

Chapter Eleven

Dinah adjusted the back of the poolside lounge chair to a more comfortable position and settled against it as the splash of divers and the shouts of children rang in her ears.

Behind the dark glasses she was wearing, she shut her eyes and sighed. Usually she avoided the pool area. She didn't need any reminders of Todd Campbell. Even though he'd gone back to Los Angeles two months ago, he still lurked in the shadow of her mind, always ready to leap full force into her conscious thoughts.

Anything could trigger him, a cold can of cola, a run-down blue car passing her on the street, even her own bed where she'd slept with him. No, make that *especially* her own bed where she'd slept with him.

Quickly she switched off that thought and opened the book she'd brought with her. A horror/fantasy. Not her favorite reading, but she still couldn't read a romance or a private eye mystery without breaking down.

It was a weakness she was making every effort to control.

She heard the lifeguard shout something, and looked up to see him standing at the side of the pool, admonishing one of the children. The guard's name was Kenny, and he was twenty-two years old with a physique almost as good as Todd's, but that's where the resemblance ended. Every swimmer in the complex had adored Todd, but she'd received numerous complaints about Kenny.

That was the only reason she'd braved the painful memories and come to spend time lounging beside the pool on this hot Saturday afternoon in September. She wanted to see for herself how he was behaving.

She watched as he scolded the child but didn't interfere. He was more harsh than she'd have liked, but the swimmers were his responsibility, and therefore he had to be free to admonish them as he saw fit.

That is, of course, unless he went too far.

She returned her attention to her book, and was just picking up the threads of the plot when an achingly familiar male voice made her heart stop beating.

"Hello, Dinah."

She dropped the book, and it fell to the cement as she looked up.

"Todd!"

Oh, my God, it wasn't just a fantasy. He was towering over her and, though he was wearing dark glasses, there was no doubting his identity. She'd have known it was him even if she'd been blind. Only he could make her go hot and cold at the same time just by saying hello.

He squatted down to pick up her book, and she quickly sat up and swung her feet to the floor. That was a mistake, because now her bare legs almost touched his, which were also bare. They were both wearing shorts.

"Wh-what are you doing here?" she asked in a voice that squeaked with surprise.

He didn't stand again but continued to hunker beside her, which put his face just inches from hers. "I came to see you," he said, and laid the book on the end of the lounge. "You wouldn't answer my calls or open my letters, so I came to try to make peace with you in person."

She couldn't see his eyes behind the glasses, and she was thankful that he couldn't see hers for the same reason, but his tone was friendly and nonthreatening, neither too intimate nor too harsh.

"You shouldn't have done that." She was relieved that her voice had almost returned to normal. "You had to have known that I didn't want any contact with you. I still don't."

That was a lie, and she knew it. She hated herself for knowing it. There could never be anything between her and this man again, and he was as aware of it as she. So why didn't he leave her alone to get over this catastrophic infatuation that even his deceit hadn't destroyed?

"I know only too well," he said, "but I'm not going to let it go at that. You have been told, haven't you, that we found the Fabergé egg in Erhardt's apartment, and the jewels were inside just as I'd suspected?"

Dinah nodded. "Yes, Officer Irwin has kept me informed. He said that Anson's parole has been revoked, and Bernie will stand trial for grand theft."

"That's right, and neither of them is talking. It's possible that you'll have to go back to Los Angeles to testify when Bernie's trial comes up."

She sighed and stood, careful not to touch him when she did. "Yes, well, I'll worry about that when, and if, it happens."

Todd rose, and Dinah walked several steps away. "I won't say it's been nice seeing you, Todd, because it hasn't. All it's done is tear open old wounds. I hope you'll have the decency not to bother me again."

She thought she saw him flinch, but she was turning to leave at the time and couldn't be sure. When he spoke again, there was no hint of sarcasm in his voice, only determination. "But, Dinah, I have no decency. You've made that clear, so don't expect me to act as if I did. I'm staying at a nearby hotel, and I'm not going to give up until you hear me out."

A sick feeling of desolation assailed her as a thought occurred to her. "Are you spying on me again?"

She had her back to him and couldn't see his expression, but his tone was gentle. "I already made that mistake once, and I not only lost your friendship and respect, but it was a waste of time.

"The only thing I learned was that you are the sweetest, most honorable and caring woman I've ever known, and I suspected that the first time we met."

The rest of the day was a disaster. Seeing Todd again had totally undone what little progress she'd made at putting that degrading episode in her life behind her. All the pain and self-analysis of the past two months, to say nothing of the self-reproach, had been a waste.

She hadn't learned a thing. Todd Campbell still had the power to make her heart pound, her hands shake and her body throb with wanting. When she'd looked up and had seen him standing there, her first impulse had been to throw her arms around him and never let him go again.

Fortunately by the next morning she'd regained some of her composure, if not her good sense, and she even managed a practice smile as she drove into the parking lot of the church. In the narthex she shook hands with the greeters and chatted for a few minutes before continuing on.

She'd gone only a few steps when someone touched her arm, and Todd's voice said, "You're looking very beautiful this morning, Dinah."

Again she was torn by the conflicting emotions of gladness and anger as she turned to look at him. What she saw made her blink. She'd never seen him so dressed up before. He was wearing a blue suit with a white dress shirt and a blue paisley tie. If possible, he looked even sexier than he did in a bathing suit or tight jeans.

With an effort, she tore her gaze away from him and noticed that all the well-dressed girls and women were looking at him admiringly as they went by.

She remembered why she was angry. "You said you weren't spying on me—"

His hand on her arm tightened. "I'm not, but I followed you here the day the baby was baptized. I came in and sat at the back, and I could see that you were a valued member of the congregation. I took a chance that you might come again this morning, and I was right. Do you mind if I sit with you?"

Her first impulse was to say yes, she did mind, but that wasn't a very nice way to behave in church. Besides, he'd admitted to having followed her in the past. At least he was open about it and apparently wasn't still lying to her.

"You can sit wherever it pleases you," she said grumpily, unwilling to appear welcoming.

He smiled and put his hand under her elbow as they walked toward the sanctuary. "It pleases me to sit with you," he said softly.

For the next hour, try as she would, Dinah couldn't keep her mind on what was going on in the service. She was too aware of Todd. He sat beside her, close but not touching, and they shared a hymnal when they sang. He had a well-trained tenor voice, and she was surprised that he knew all the hymns without stumbling.

He must have noticed, because after the second one he leaned over and whispered, "My family went to church every Sunday when I was growing up, and I sang in the choir when I was in high school. I'm sorry to say I got out of the habit once I went away to college."

While the minister delivered the sermon, Dinah's attention kept straying to the man beside her. It would be easier for her if he weren't so handsome, but the love she felt for him was far more than just surface attraction.

Todd seemed to be everything she'd ever wanted in a man. He was bright, ambitious, had a good sense of humor and was a sensitive but passionate lover.

The only things missing were a standard of morals and a sense of honor, the most important traits of all. Without them the other attributes were worthless. A man like that would leave a string of broken hearts everywhere he went, and Dinah's poor trusting heart had already been broken twice. Once more, and it would never survive.

When the service was over, they were stopped several times on the way out by friends of Dinah's wanting to welcome her companion. She introduced him as a friend of the family from out of state who was passing through and stopped to see her.

After the third time she did it, he nudged her and whispered, "Don't you know it's a sin to lie in church?"

She cocked one eyebrow and whispered back. "It's not exactly a lie. I know you'd like my parents if you ever met them."

He looked straight into her eyes. "I intend to meet them, and soon."

They walked together to the parking lot. "Do you have car?" she asked as they stopped beside her red Toyota.

"Over there." He motioned toward a new shiny black Corvette. It had a California license plate, so she knew it was his and not a rental.

"My, you have come up in the world," she said, and here was bitterness in her tone. "How you must have hated that poor little wreck you drove when you were here before."

She looked at him and felt humiliated all over again. "And it's not only your car that's been upscaled. That suit has to have been custom-made to fit so perfectly. Unless I'm badly mistaken, the material is silk."

"Silk blend," he muttered, "but don't forget, I was drawing two paychecks while I was here. One from you, and one from the firm."

Her short laugh was taunting. "What I paid you wouldn't even buy the suit, let alone the car. How did you really get through college, Todd? It wasn't by working as a lifeguard. Did Daddy pay your expenses?"

His expression remained passive, as did his voice. "Most of them, yes, but you're wrong about one thing. I did work summers as a lifeguard."

He shifted his stance. "You have a right to be resentful of my deviousness, Dinah. I accept that, and I deeply regret that it was necessary, but I'm not going to apologize for making a decent wage at my chosen profession. I work hard, and I have no one to spend my money on but myself."

She felt a stab of shame. Her belligerence was only making matters worse. "I'm sorry," she said, and looked away from him. "Of course you should be proud of being successful. It just...well, it hurts to know how gullible and naive I was. I actually worried about you spending money on me! You must have had a good laugh when I insisted on paying my own way all the time.''

"Laugh!" His hands landed on her shoulders and turned her around to face him. His expression was livid. "You think I was laughing at you? Dinah, it took all the control I had to keep from crying. You were so sweet and considerate, and I hated what I was doing to you. I knew I was setting us both up for just this type of grief when you found out about me."

Before she realized what he was going to do, he pulled her to him and wrapped her in his arms. "I can't tell you how many times I vowed to quit. To tell my boss to send somebody else to do the dirty work. To confess that I was too personally involved with you to continue."

He'd startled her by taking her in his arms, and she trembled as their bodies pressed together in an electrifying oneness. This was madness! She couldn't surrender to him. She had to remember that he was a charming con man who had no scruples about how he got what he wanted.

Right now he still wanted her, probably because she'd sent him away and he wasn't used to that, but his attention span was short. Who would he want next week? Or next month?

Putting her palms on his chest, she pushed away from him and glared. "But you didn't quit, did you? You conveniently overcame your qualms and continued to probe and pry and seduce me until you found out what you wanted to know."

Todd's fist clenched and unclenched in frustration. "I didn't ask to be recalled because it wouldn't have ended there. They'd have sent another operative, someone older and more experienced who would do the job and not give a damn how his methods might affect you."

He ran his hand through his hair and looked away from er. "I couldn't stand the thought of another man watch-g you, learning your personal habits, going through your ings and putting a negative interpretation on everything ou did.

"No, Dinah, I didn't quit. I know you won't believe is, but I stayed on to protect you."

The truly scary thing was that she did believe it. She houldn't. There was no reason for her to. He'd admitted deceiving her about almost everything, but for some eason she was sure he was telling her the truth this time.

Was it because of his sincerity or because she wanted to elieve so badly?

Abruptly she opened the car door and slid into the driv-r's seat. Todd leaned down and put his hands on the open indowsill.

"Don't run off," he said. "Meet me somewhere for unch. There's a restaurant in my hotel that serves excel-ent food—"

"No," she said, and started the motor. "Thank you, but o."

He continued to hang on to the window with one hand vhile he reached inside his suit coat with the other and withdrew several envelopes held together with a rubber and. "All right, but please take these with you and read hem."

He handed her the stack, and she recognized them as the etters he'd written her over the past two months. She'd eturned them all unopened.

She caught her breath and tried to hand them back to im. "No, I—"

He ignored them. "Please, Dinah. Even a serial mur-lerer is entitled to a fair trial. You stuck by your husband until he was convicted of grand theft, but I haven't even broken the law.''

His voice was raw with emotion. ''You won't listen to my side so, please, read about it. It's all written down in those letters, all the things I did and everything I felt. If, after you've read them and judged them fairly, you still want nothing more to do with me, then I'll go back to L.A. and never trouble you again, but at least give me a chance.''

She was swayed by the pleading in his tone. She doubted that Todd Campbell had ever pleaded for anything before in his life, and she couldn't ignore it.

Hesitantly she put the envelopes on the passenger seat and shoved the transmission into reverse. ''All right, Todd,'' she said shakily. ''If it means that much to you, but I doubt that it will change anything.''

''Maybe not,'' he said, ''but I'll know I did everything I could. I've written the name of my hotel and the phone number on the back of the first envelope. Call me when you've finished reading.''

Back home Dinah tossed the stack of letters on the coffee table with all the disinterest she could muster. She would read them because she'd promised Todd she would, but she wasn't going to be in any hurry about it. He could darn well wait.

The problem was that she couldn't. Those envelopes might as well have been equipped with a loud beeper that went off every few minutes. No matter how hard she tried, she couldn't keep her mind off them.

She'd had no desire to read each of them when they'd arrived at regular intervals after Todd went back to Los Angeles, and she'd returned them immediately, but now they were like a magnet drawing her inexplicably into their field.

Finally, in the early evening, she couldn't resist any longer and ripped open the first one. It began with, *My dearest love,* and she felt a lump rise in her throat.

By the time she'd finished the last one, her tears were flowing freely and blurring the ink. The letters were beautiful beyond description. Todd certainly didn't need a Cyrano de Bergerac to plead for him. There was a poetic quality about his way of putting words together that she'd never suspected he had.

He told her of his initial reluctance to accept the case, of his almost immediate attraction to her, and even of the doubts that had tormented him. He explained that far from seducing her to gain her trust, he'd actually held back, much to his physical and emotional distress, because he knew that's what she'd think he'd done once she learned the truth about him.

He said he loved her, but could she believe him? He'd lied to her about so many things. Wouldn't it be better just to tell him she'd forgiven him and send him away?

But what if he was telling the truth?

She swiped at her wet cheeks with the back of her hands and stood up. There was only one way to find out. A telephone call wouldn't do it. She had to confront him face-to-face.

Twenty minutes later, Dinah stood in front of the door marked 805 in the luxury hotel and knocked. Her knees were shaking, and her stomach was tied in knots. What if he wasn't here? Worse, what if he was? What was she going to say?

She knocked again, and a voice from within called, "Who is it?"

She cleared her throat. "It's Dinah."

The door was opened almost immediately, and Todd stood before her, dressed in the familiar faded jeans and a T-shirt. Once again he was the carefree young lifeguard she'd found so irresistible, and she almost turned and ran.

For a moment he didn't move, but his gaze scrutinized every inch of her face. "You've been crying," he said tenderly, and stepped back to let her in.

"Yes," she said, and swallowed back a stray sob.

"You read the letters?"

"Yes."

He put up his hand and touched her tear-swollen cheek. "Why did they make you cry?"

She'd been wrong. He wasn't her carefree lifeguard anymore. This Todd was no boy, but a man beset with guilt and doubts. His uncertainty showed in his face, and agony looked out of his eyes.

"B-because they were so wonderfully sensitive," she said just before he put his arms around her and cradled her against him.

"Every word in them was the truth." He rubbed his cheek in her hair. "You do believe that, don't you?"

She put her arms around his waist and inhaled his musky male scent as she laid her head on his shoulder. "I . . . yes, I guess I do."

"Guess isn't good enough," he said sadly. "This is too important. You either believe me or you don't. It can't be halfway, love."

Dinah knew he was right. She had good reason to doubt him, but he'd only been doing his job. There was no need for him to go to such lengths to win her forgiveness unless he really did care for her.

She kissed the side of his neck, then tasted it with her tongue. "I believe you, my darling, and I love you, maybe 'not wisely,' as Shakespeare put it, 'but too well.'"

Todd had shivered when she'd caressed him with her tongue, but now he stepped back, causing her to raise her head and look at him. "What do you mean by 'not wisely'?" he demanded. "If you still don't trust me—"

"Oh, no, Todd, that's not what I meant," she said anxiously. "It's just that...well, taking a lover could never be really 'wise' for me, but I love you too well not to."

He frowned. "What's this talk about taking a lover? I don't want to be your part-time lover, Dinah, I want to be your full-time husband."

She blinked. "Husband! You want to *marry* me?"

His frown disappeared, and he chuckled as he drew her close again. "Of course I want to marry you. What in hell did you think I was talking about in those letters?"

"Well, you said you needed me, wanted me with you, but marriage? I'm older than you."

"Oh my God, are we back to that again?" he groaned. "What possible difference can seven years make? It just means that we'll have even more time together. A woman's life span is longer than a man's, so you probably won't be left an elderly widow." He grinned. "We'll spend our old age together."

Put that way it really didn't seem to be much of an obstacle, but there was another, more pressing, reason why she shouldn't marry him. He apparently hadn't thought of it, and for a moment she considered not mentioning it, but her sense of fair play wouldn't let her.

"Todd," she said hesitantly. "I may not be able to give you children."

He lowered his head and nuzzled the side of her neck. "I know," he murmured softly. "You told me about the problem with infertility in your marriage, but it doesn't matter, sweetheart. Being a father isn't high on my list of priorities."

He was being sweet, but she couldn't accept that great of a sacrifice. "Maybe not now it isn't," she pointed out, "but in another ten years it might be. You're entitled to sons and daughters to carry on your family genes."

He raised his head again and looked at her. "I have a brother and two sisters to do that," he reminded her. "I'm entitled to happiness, too, and you are my happiness, Dinah. You're my joy, and my hope, and my dreams for the future. Without you there are nothing but empty years stretching ahead. I know. I've had two months of that particular hell, and I don't think I could face any more of it."

She felt the stirrings of exhilaration. "You mean you've felt that way, too? Oh, darling, I've been so bereft without you. It all seemed so hopeless. I love you so much...."

A smile of sheer exuberance split his face. "Then what are we standing here arguing about, woman? Say you'll marry me so we can get to the kissing."

Her exhilaration escalated as she lifted her face to his. "When you put it that way, what can I say but yes?" she said happily. "Oh, yes, Todd, I'll marry you, and about that kissing—"

"Don't tell me—show me," he said just before his mouth settled hungrily over hers.

And she did.

*   *   *   *   *

FOUR UNIQUE SERIES
FOR EVERY WOMAN YOU ARE...

Silhouette Romance®

Tender, delightful, provocative—stories that capture the laughter, the tears, the *joy* of falling in love. Pure romance...straight from the heart!

SILHOUETTE *Desire*®

Go wild with Desire! Passionate, emotional, sensuous stories of fiery romance. With heroines you'll like and heroes you'll *love*, Silhouette Desire never fails to deliver.

Silhouette Special Edition®

Stories of love and life, these powerful novels are tales that you can identify with—romances with "something special" added in! Silhouette Special Edition is entertainment for the heart.

SILHOUETTE·INTIMATE·MOMENTS®

Enter a world where passions run hot and excitement is the rule. Dramatic, larger-than-life and always compelling—Silhouette Intimate Moments will never let you down.